PENGUIN METRO READS
THE SECRETS WE KEEP

Sudeep Nagarkar has authored ten bestselling novels and has been featured on the *Forbes India* longlist of the most influential celebrities for three consecutive years. He was also awarded 'Celebrity Author of 2013' by Amazon India. In 2016, he was awarded 'Youth Icon of India' by Zee Awards and the WBR group.

He also writes for television and has given guest lectures at institutes such as the IITs and for organizations like TEDx.

Connect with Sudeep via his:
Facebook fan page: sudeepnagarkar
Facebook profile: nagarkarsudeep
Twitter: sudeep_nagarkar
Instagram: sudeepnagarkar

BY THE SAME AUTHOR

Few Things Left Unsaid
That's the Way We Met
It Started with a Friend Request
Sorry, You're Not My Type
You're the Password to My Life
You're Trending in My Dreams
All Rights Reserved for You
She Swiped Right into My Heart
Our Story Needs No Filter
She Friend-Zoned My Love

Sudeep Nagarkar

the secrets we keep

Penguin
metro reads

An imprint of Penguin Random House

PENGUIN METRO READS

USA | Canada | UK | Ireland | Australia
New Zealand | India | South Africa | China

Penguin Metro Reads is part of the Penguin Random House group of companies
whose addresses can be found at global.penguinrandomhouse.com

Published by Penguin Random House India Pvt. Ltd
7th Floor, Infinity Tower C, DLF Cyber City,
Gurgaon 122 002, Haryana, India

Penguin
Random House
India

First published in Penguin Metro Reads by Penguin Random House India 2019

Copyright © Sudeep Nagarkar 2019

ISBN 9789385990014

Typeset in Adobe Caslon Pro by Manipal Digital Systems, Manipal
Printed at Thomson Press India Ltd, New Delhi

www.penguin.co.in

MIX
Paper
FSC   FSC® C010615

Prologue

If you could forget a relationship that fleetingly existed in the past, would you? If your past could be erased, would you erase it?

Sadly, you have no choice in this matter because I—your past—am invincible.

Mysterious and unseen, I am the master of the dark and light and everything in between. I am a force of nature, an unstoppable wave that'll tame you by taking away every last bit of your strength, until you regret ever standing in my path. A king of manipulation at its finest, I will see into the soul of the characters in this story long before they catch a glimpse, and change the way they think. I am the only God and the only devil, and I am here to destroy you because without destruction there's no creation.

If you think you can escape me, you're already doomed.

Prologue

Chapter 1

The house was a two-storey building surrounded by palm trees. The main feature of the dining room was a large oak table around which a family sat, enjoying their dinner. The family consisted of Akriti and her parents. To potential onlookers, they seemed happy, taking bites of their food and exchanging smiling glances with each other. The father paused after a bite and cleared his throat, 'This is about his family. Where are they and why are they silent? We can't just allow things to proceed without an assurance from them.'

Before Akriti could answer, the sound of a fork banging on a plate caused them to turn to face her mother. 'After all, it's your happiness that matters the most to us, but for that we have to make sure you are in the right hands.'

Akriti made her way towards her room on the upper floor and slammed the door. She leaned against it and closed her eyes. Her face was pale with exhaustion and fatigue. She turned to place her ear against the door. Her parents were still arguing. These days they were always arguing, and most of the time she was their subject. She shook her head and began changing into her nightclothes to sleep the awful night away. As she walked towards the bed, she thought she heard a noise above her head. The house did not have an attic, so at first the sound confused her, and then alerted her when she heard another and then another. It sounded like footsteps on her roof heading to her parents' bedroom.

She froze, not moving until the sounds were farther away from her. She took a deep breath, switched off the lights and quickly walked to her parents' bedroom, where they were still arguing behind their own closed door. She raised a hand to knock when, all of a sudden, she heard the sound of breaking glass, her mother's screams and a gunshot. Her eyes filled with tears as she registered what could have taken place.

'Find the girl,' a deep, muffled voice ordered.

Frightened, Akriti rushed to her room, once more closing the door behind her. She frantically looked around for a place to hide. She considered hiding under the bed but went into her closet instead, closing her eyes and praying for a miracle. She held her breath and willed her heart to stop pounding, when she heard her room door opening and the soft footsteps of an intruder entering her private space. Beads of sweat dripped down the sides of her face as the stranger walked towards her bed, lifting the delicate bedspread to see if she was hiding underneath.

'Rahul?' a man's voice called from the hallway.

'Here,' the voice from the room answered.

'Her parents are in the master bedroom,' the voice from the hallway said. It sounded familiar but she didn't dare come out.

'I flashed my torchlight and alarmed the two bad guys, but . . . we were too late. They . . .'

She strained her ears to hear more of the conversation, but it seemed curiously muffled. She stood and pressed her ear to the door of the closet, holding her breath and waiting for whatever was going to happen next. A few moments later, she let out a breath, inhaling the darkness and trying to make sense of the events that had just taken place. She reached for the doorknob, when suddenly, it was yanked open and she stood staring at two men holding handguns. As the men realized who they were pointing their guns at, they relaxed and lowered them. Stepping back, they stood looking at each other.

When Akriti realized the two men were Rahul and his friend, Neerav, she instinctively hugged Rahul.

'There is nothing to worry about. Your parents are okay. However, we didn't manage to apprehend the guys. I am sure they were associated with the same mission. Neerav was keeping an eye on your house, so we were able to get here in time.'

'Why are they trying to kill me?' Akriti was still out of breath.

'You'll have to come with us. Only you. Not your parents,' Rahul ordered, ignoring her question. Her parents, who were now standing unharmed next to Akriti, stared at each other with blank expressions.

'What's happening and where are you taking her?' Akriti's dad was worried. There were so many questions he did not have the answer to.

~

Akriti sat at a table with Rahul and Neerav by her side. The room was cold and lifeless. The entire area resembled an isolation camp. The meeting room—the one she was currently seated in—had only steel tables, a few chairs and a large screen on the wall. The screen in front of them flickered on, and Akriti found herself staring at a face that could only belong to a person of authority, judging by his stern demeanour.

'Good job, team. This is not an easy task, considering we do not know why these events are happening. There could be spy agencies involved. Although I would have preferred that you had got hold of those attackers, it is good to know that the entire family is safe.'

'Director Rajiv Jain,' Rahul addressed the screen, 'Akriti's parents are not in town for the next half of the month. They are leaving for Jaipur tomorrow to attend a family wedding. Since Akriti is going to be alone, it would be in her best interests if she were somewhere safer.'

The director thought for a moment before asking, 'Do you have a location in mind, Rahul?'

Rahul nodded.

'You might as well go ahead, then. Remember, her safety is our primary concern. If necessary, take some time off. Is that clear?'

'As crystal, Director. Thank you.'

The man on the screen disappeared. Rahul sighed with relief, lost in his thoughts for a brief moment before realizing Neerav and Akriti were staring at him in wonder.

'What?' he snarled at them.

'Where are you taking me without my permission?' Akriti raised her eyebrows.

'To my house.'

'Your house? Are you serious? When was the last time you visited your house or even spoke to your family?' Akriti scanned his face, searching for answers, as she knew that Rahul was not on speaking terms with his family. Rahul held her by her shoulders and looked into her eyes.

'Now that I have some time on my hands, I want us to take the next step in our relationship.'

Neerav had a grin on his face.

'That is out of character for you, Officer Rahul, considering we have company,' Akriti teased, indicating Neerav's presence.

'Do we?' Rahul smiled, his eyes locked on Akriti's face. In his mind, he contemplated how long it had been since he'd left his house.

It had, indeed, been a very long time.

～

I was wrong. We were all wrong. We should've stopped him, but we didn't. We should've persuaded him to stay. Perhaps he would've stayed. There are so many questions I shall never find answers to. The house, in his absence, is silent from the sadness that follows separation. Today, I don't know where Rahul is. My faith in you, my God, is divine, and I know you will keep him happy wherever he is. Even if he wishes to come back, we have left him no place to return. These days, I stay up all night thinking about him; picturing him as a little boy.

It was through her prayers that his mother wished to reach out to Rahul. She wasn't aware that her son, who had left fifteen years ago never to return, was already on his way back home. The Rahul who'd left was a fourteen-year-old impulsive kid who had brought disgrace to his family. He'd never been able to match his brother's excellence in his studies. Instead, his churlish behaviour had been everybody's concern. In contrast, the Rahul who was returning was an intelligence officer with a reputation for undertaking the riskiest missions, calmly and tactically.

Everything about him had changed; the city, however, remained the same. Rahul was lost in thought when he rang the doorbell. Raju, the caretaker, opened the door but didn't recognize him.

'How can I help you?' Raju asked. Instead of answering, Rahul entered the house and searched for his mother, who was working in the kitchen.

He had forgotten the rage he had felt when he left years ago, and now, as he called out to his mother, his voice sounded as though it belonged to an infant.

'Mummy . . . Mummy . . .' he called for his mom till he entered the kitchen and saw her. 'How have you been? You recognize me, don't you?'

'Rahul?'

'Where are the others? Dad? Karan?'

Everyone in the house gathered around Rahul to witness his return. It was, indeed, true. The younger son had returned, and while his mother was beaming with excitement, his father did not seem very pleased. Mr Rane was not a man easily swayed by emotions. He eyed Rahul suspiciously. If his son had returned after fifteen long years, there was bound to be an underlying purpose. That purpose, Mr Rane intended to find out.

'Am I daydreaming, Rahul?' Mr Rane feigned surprise. Rahul simply smiled and touched his feet.

'I cannot believe my eyes. I must go to the temple today to thank God for answering my prayers after all these years. Where were you all this time?' his mother had tears in her eyes.

'Yes, where is your house?' His father's questions sounded more like an interrogation.

'I haven't bought one yet. I rent places and keep moving, because who knows where I'll be the next day? Owning a house requires maintenance. I am currently staying in a rented flat in Delhi. Before that, I was in Shivpuri. Like all kids who abandon their families at a young age, I, too, have seen terrible times.' There was sadness in Rahul's laughter.

'I am sorry. I should have stopped you,' said his father.

'You don't have to be. I may have gone away in a fit of rage but, at the end of it all, I am happy.'

'So, what do you do for a living?' his father asked curiously.

'I am working with the Intelligence Network Agency (INA).'

8

That seemed to startle everybody. No one had expected Rahul to be working with an organization as prestigious as the INA. His mother's pride was inevitable. His father, however, showed little reaction. What Rahul's smile did not convey was his disappointment. He had been disappointed with his family for never bothering to search for him, never caring to reach out to him, let alone persuading him to return. The doorbell rang to announce the arrival of Rahul's elder brother, Karan. As Raju opened the door, he told Karan that there was a surprise waiting for him.

'I know. Dad messaged me,' Karan replied.

'Karan, how are you?' Rahul asked.

Karan gave a slight smile but did not bother to answer. Rahul was not surprised. In the years he'd spent with Karan, there was nothing worth remembering. Whenever the brothers were together, their father made it a point to compare the two. These frequent comparisons distanced Rahul from Karan. For his part, Karan looked down on his younger brother and never objected to his father's derisive remarks. Eventually, the rift between them was large enough to part them emotionally. After eating the lunch prepared by his mother, Rahul passed out on the sofa. His father was sitting in his chair having a cup of tea and gazing at the sky through the window, when Karan asked him, 'Why is Rahul here after so many years?'

'I am sure he is here for some selfish reason. If it were for the love of his family, he would have returned long ago. We should talk to him and find out more.' His dad took a last sip before putting his cup on the side table. Cleaning his specs, he added, 'Tomorrow we are meeting the girl's family for your marriage. See to it that Rahul doesn't cause any sort of disruption. You know him and his old ways.'

'Yes, Dad.' Karan began walking towards his room. He stopped midway and quietly opened the door of the room where Rahul slept. There had to be a reason why his brother had bothered to remember his family after all this time.

As soon as his brother left the room, Rahul retrieved his phone from his pocket and texted Akriti, who along with Neerav, was staying at a hotel nearby.

You can check out from the hotel tomorrow afternoon. I plan on telling my parents about you in the morning. I am not sure they'll be too pleased about it.

Akriti was amused by the fact that an intelligence officer would be so rattled about confronting his parents.

All the best for the mission, Officer. She smiled at the other end.

Chapter 2

Not everyone was thrilled about Rahul's return. Mr Rane, for instance, tried to ignore his son. Not only had his son not bothered to apologize, but he also wore the same defiant expression as when he had left. Rahul, on the other hand, was nervous about confronting his family with the reason for his arrival. He knew he would have never returned if the mission hadn't required their cooperation. But now that he had, he knew he'd missed his mother's smile, and perhaps he'd missed the air of this city as well.

'Raju kaka, why is everyone getting dressed up? Is there supposed to be a function today?' asked Rahul the next morning at the breakfast table.

'Oh baba, don't you know? Talks of Karan bhaiya's marriage are going on, and the girl, along with her family, is coming to see us today,' Raju answered, before rushing into the kitchen to continue with the arrangements.

'Love marriage, is it?' Rahul teased, picking up the banana that was on the table.

Mr Rane, who was seated in his chair overlooking the window, responded with authority, 'Arranged. There is no such thing as love marriage. It's either arranged or you choose to defy principles.'

After a pregnant silence, Rahul spoke to his mother in a disapproving tone, 'He hasn't changed a bit, has he? Still interfering with our lives to prove his dominance. Even after all these years, he continues to enforce his orthodox beliefs. If he chose the wrong partner for me, would he be accountable for the mistake?'

'The girl is coming to see Karan, not you. And Karan is okay with that. Now don't create a fuss, please,' his mother retorted.

'Why would Karan object? He's always been the perfect son to both of you. If obeying your draconian principles meant losing perspective, Karan would happily do that as well.'

'Stop being difficult. Maybe we're happy believing what we have always believed,' his mother tried to placate him.

'This is primarily why I left. In this family, nobody really cares about how you feel. All they care about is that you don't mar their reputation built on irrational beliefs,' Rahul was furious.

'Please, Rahul, try not to create a scene in front of everyone today. The girl's family will be arriving any moment now. Go and get ready.'

'Anyhow, they are not here to see *me*,' he said with indifference.

After Mrs Rane had left, his father turned to Rahul, 'Don't come after more than a decade and try to change our way of living.'

Mr Rane was dressed in a kurta pyjama that only reinforced his authoritative persona. Rahul left the living room to avoid any more arguments. Even after his professional accomplishments, it wasn't as if his opinion was regarded.

What was the point of the rules if they only created a rift in the family? Traditions, religions and beliefs did not define a happy family; affection and understanding did. Perhaps, then, theirs would never be a happy family.

~

The Pathak family was supposed to have come by lunchtime but was already an hour late. Karan had drunk two cups of tea out of anxiety. Rahul, on the other hand, was indifferently watching television.

'Are they even coming? Have you tried calling them?' Rahul asked Karan, who was busy tucking in his shirt in front of the mirror.

'Dad tried calling Mr Pathak but his phone was not reachable. You know the traffic during rush hours,' Karan replied, not looking away from the mirror.

As time passed, the restlessness was visible on everyone's face, except Rahul's, as he continued watching television.

'Rahul, switch it off and change your clothes! They could arrive any time now,' his mother shouted.

'It's been more than an hour and a half. Plus, I am comfortable in my shorts,' he casually replied, as he surfed through channels to find something interesting to watch.

'I suppose you would have absolutely no problem wearing just your underwear as well then,' his mom continued yelling.

'First of all, they are shorts. And second, I don't think they are coming.'

Karan looked frustrated. He had been looking forward to meeting this girl and her parents. Karan, who spent each penny in his wallet judiciously, had bought his shirt from the most expensive store in the city. *What a complete waste!* he thought.

'You can wear it to my wedding,' Rahul teased, reading his thoughts, 'and I am sure my wife will make it on time.'

The moment the bell rang, Rahul rushed into the kitchen with the pants he was supposed to wear. The Pathak family, along with their daughter, Rashi, entered the house.

'Sorry we are late. With traffic, you never know,' Mr Pathak smiled apologetically.

'Don't worry, it's fine,' Mrs Rane said.

Once everyone had settled and tea was served, both the families shared an awkward silence, until they saw Rahul emerging from the kitchen.

'Hello, everyone. Sorry, I was getting ready.'

Mr Rane gave Rahul a dirty look before turning back to Mr Pathak and smiling. Mrs Rane signalled Rahul to zip his pants. She called for Karan, who had rushed to check himself in the mirror one last time.

'So, this is our son, Karan. He is an MBA graduate and senior executive in one of the most prominent business firms in India, Reliance Industries.'

'Now that I think of it, shouldn't it have been the other way round? Custom dictates that it's the boy's family that visits the girl's family. Considering how committed families are these days to customs,' Rahul had a tone of ridicule in his voice, 'how come you got this one wrong?'

'Rahul, please stop talking nonsense so we can discuss what we are here for,' Rahul's mother dodged the question.

'Aunty, I think his question is valid.' Rashi spoke for the first time, 'It was I who insisted we meet the boy's family. Since it is the girl who comes to stay with the boy's family after marriage, I suggested it was better I saw the place I was to live in. I found it illogical the other way round. Is that a good enough answer, Mr . . .'

'Rahul,' Rahul smiled.

'So, I was telling you about our son, Karan, Mr Pathak,' Mr Rane tried to change the subject. 'We have raised Karan very traditionally.'

'Ah, now that's the indicator of a reputable family.'

'And being reputable is not the most important thing, Mr Pathak,' Rahul added.

'I appreciate your thoughts, Mr Rahul, but can we hear from Karan? We might as well switch roles, Karan, since you are shying away like a girl,' Rashi tried to joke.

Everyone, except Mr Rane, laughed. He was getting a little upset with Rashi's upfront nature.

Rahul sensed it and suggested that both Karan and Rashi be given some private space, to which everyone agreed. After the two left for Karan's room, the elders continued discussing the importance of tradition. 'It is hard to find a family that is respected and values tradition. We are also against the concept of love marriage. These days, children lack maturity and get married without consulting their parents, which explains why so many marriages end in divorce.'

'Sir, that is not the case. Love marriages involve mutual understanding and respect between the couple. Also, not getting divorced hardly implies that the marriage is successful. People choose to stay in an unhappy marriage, mostly because they are too afraid to separate, keeping in mind the ideals of the society. The couple getting married should be content about the decision; be it love or arranged. Don't you think some traditions should change with time?'

'So, are you looking for a girl for Rahul too?' Mr Pathak asked, ignoring everything that Rahul had just said.

'Yes . . . we are,' his mom answered.

'Why would you lie? They will not be looking for a girl for me. I already have someone in my life, and I shall marry her when it pleases me. Her name is Akriti. You older people can go on and on with your litany of customs and principles but it will have no effect on me. You'll never realize how hollow these words sound.'

No one knew the argument would escalate so quickly. The Pathak family decided not to take things any further and they left. Mr Rane was sorry his younger son had turned a fateful meeting into a debacle. Without disrespecting each other, they signed off. Karan was clueless as to why the Pathak family had left in such haste, but he knew that whatever had happened had something to do with Rahul. Mr Rane quietly sat on his chair while Rahul's mom sobbed alone in her room. In the midst of all the chaos, Rahul had forgotten to call Akriti. He rushed to his room to check his phone. The screen showed numerous missed calls from both Akriti and Neerav. Akriti was going to kill him for his reckless attitude. Considering the circumstances, he decided to call her when things calmed down a bit.

As Rahul walked back into the living room, his father was waiting to confront him.

'Why are you here? You didn't bother to try to contact us all these years and now you are here, all of a sudden, acting as if everything were normal.'

Rahul stayed quiet but his father continued, 'Are you here for money? For your house, perhaps? If that's the case, please take the money and leave. You are only doing to us what you did fifteen years back—damaging our reputation and bringing us shame.'

'Dad, I think we should let Rahul speak . . .' Karan interrupted, trying to ease the situation, but he was made to shut up.

Rahul simply walked away to his room, upset over the entire situation. This time, Karan followed him to his room and made him sit. This sudden change in Karan's behaviour surprised Rahul, but he was too disturbed to speak.

'Calm down, Rahul. You know Dad. You cannot change his perception of the world. Your ideology may be different, perhaps much better than his, but you cannot bring him around to see the world through your eyes.'

'I am not here to seek anything. Why won't he understand? Why did I feel the need to run away? Because I was left with no choice.'

'We have lived our lives in a certain way for too long to change their course now. What happened with you . . . the reasons why you ran . . . your troubles and predicaments . . . nobody knows them well enough to understand them. Dad and Mom are clueless about how troubled you were. I was aware of your situation, but you barely bothered to confront us with it. I know what happened that day. I know the exact reason behind your decision to run away. You could have resolved it. Instead, you chose to run. Just like that, without saying anything.'

'You knew why I had done it?' Rahul raised his eyebrows.

'Yes, but I never spoke about it to anyone.'

Rahul smiled sadly. Karan put a comforting arm on his shoulder. Rahul could not remember when they'd last been like that.

In the process of growing up, the child in us is often left confused and silenced, without answers. But even after all these years, we are still the same child, with a few more scars.

Chapter 3

Eighteen years ago

Rahul did not want to try to be perfect but he had little choice. When your older sibling excels in school, has a good rapport with teachers, is praised for his behaviour, and all you happen to be is a notorious urchin, you feel defeated. So you try to be your older sibling, replicating his style around your family, in an attempt to woo their hearts. But you fail every time because your parents won't accept anything less than a prodigy. And that, however hard you try, you cannot be. All Rahul wanted was for his parents to love him for the person he already was, not the person they wanted him to be.

'That's my fourth point. Just one to go,' Rahul punched the air after knocking Sandy's pen off the table by hitting it with his pen.

'Look, I already told you in the beginning that you are playing with a Parker pen and I have a Reynolds. Yours is a heavyweight pen and that's cheating,' Sandy said, disappointed.

'Don't cry like a child. Gear up for the next round. I am not changing my pen.'

It was Friday, and it was the day Rahul enjoyed the most. According to the dumb shuffling policy, Rahul only got to sit on the last bench on Fridays. Far from the teacher's eyes, Rahul would play all the games he could without getting noticed by the teacher, his favourite one being pen fight.

Rahul was just bending down to pick up his pen from under his desk when he caught a glimpse of the teacher's feet right in front of him.

Shit! Shit! I knocked off my pen and now she is going to knock me out of the class. Can't the bell just ring? These dreadfully long periods don't end when I want them to.

He gradually looked up towards the teacher and stood up respectfully.

'Sorry, Miss.'

'It's too bad India doesn't have a sport called pen fight. I suggest you concentrate, instead, on the fights that took place in history. The real fights—the wars.'

And I suggest you concentrate on the fights between you and your husband, so you don't have to pour your pent-up anger on your students, thought Rahul.

'Now hurry up, show me your remark notebook,' the teacher ordered.

'Please, Miss. I won't do it again. Give me one last chance, please,' Rahul begged with an innocent face.

But his pleading was in vain, and after the teacher left his side to resume teaching, there was a new remark on a page of his remark notebook in a series of remarks. He turned to look at Sandy who was grinning shamelessly. He'd got a remark from the teacher too. What was he so happy about?

'Aren't you scared to get this remark signed by your parents?' Rahul whispered. He thought to himself, *Once again, I'll spend a Sunday getting compared to Karan in every possible way.*

'No. Why do I have to show it to my parents? I am an expert in forging my mother's signature. Try it,' Sandy winked.

Rahul considered Sandy's advice for a long time before nodding his head in agreement. He would do anything to skip the harassment that followed a remark.

Pen fights were not the best thing about Friday. It was also sports day at school, and even though Rahul performed poorly in class, he was his grade's best performer in sports. He always got first prize when it came to races.

'Bro, we gotta win today. We gotta show section A that they'd rather sit at home than race with us dudes,' Sandy said, trying to sound cool. Sandy had never run a race.

'I'll try my best.' Rahul stared at the track that ran the whole length of his school's playground. He knew he was going to win. He always won. The sports teacher whistled for them to take their ready position. She held a flag in her hand and said, 'Set.' After a brief pause, she shouted, 'Go', and everybody took off.

What Rahul loved most about running was that when he ran, he left his uncertainties behind. It was like chasing the wind with playful feet. So when Rahul ran, he did not think about winning; he thought about losing himself, and then, in a moment, he would have finished the race, and he would only realize because the crowd would shout his name and clap, simultaneously. That day, he claimed the first place again. Flaunting the medal by wearing it around his neck, he reached home only to realize that he had a remark to get signed. His excitement vanished and his face became sullen. He locked himself in his room and debated whether to follow Sandy's advice.

'Rahul, first have your lunch, then do whatever you want to,' his mother called out.

'Mom, I am studying. I have my test tomorrow,' he shouted back.

'Quit lying and eat your food. Since when did you care about tests?'

'Tell Karan to eat first.'

'He already had his lunch and left for tuitions. He doesn't waste time on sports competitions,' his mother scoffed.

'I won a medal today.'

'Don't you think we'll be more proud when you come first in class? Karan stood first in the entire section last semester.'

'Ask Karan to sit for my exams as well. Good for me.'

Rahul had been practising his mother's signature all this time. He tried to replicate it by comparing it with the previous signatures in his remark notebook. He had to get it right because getting a remark was not as bad as getting caught forging your parent's signature. After multiple attempts, he succeeded in getting his mother's signature right.

The rest of the day was spent in carefully avoiding his parents. The next day in school, Rahul reluctantly showed his remark notebook to the teacher. The teacher, on close inspection, discovered that the signature had been forged. She berated Rahul for his audacity to commit such an offence. She immediately summoned his parents, asking them to meet her during lunchtime.

Rahul was petrified. He was also sad because Sandy had gotten away with his crime. His mother arrived a little before lunchtime and saw Rahul kneeling down in the corridor as a punishment.

'What have you done this time?' she asked angrily.

After the bell rang, the teacher appeared in the corridor. She suggested that Rahul and his mother come with her to her cabin. That walk to the cabin felt like the longest walk of his life. He could see dread lurking behind the cabin door.

'Sorry to bother you, Ma'am, but I am tired of Rahul's antics. Do you know Rahul got a remark for misbehaving in the class yesterday?'

Rahul's mom raised her eyebrows at Rahul, and her furious look made him sweat.

'No, he didn't tell me anything. All he said was that his test was scheduled for today and he had to prepare for it.'

'Well, there was no test scheduled for today. I am sure this is one of the many lies your child has been telling you. Anyhow, your child forged your signature on the remark I wrote in his notebook.' His teacher continued, 'I wanted to inform you, with much displeasure, that if anything like this happens again, I will be bound to take strict action.'

Rahul had reached a dead end and there was no cheat code to escape. When they reached home, his mother slapped his face. Karan tried to stop her from hitting Rahul, but she was too furious to listen to anybody.

'You think you are very smart—coming home with some complaint or other every day. You should be concentrating on your studies, but you are whiling away your time in useless sports. Do you want to be called a loser for the rest of your life? For God's sake, learn something from your elder brother!' Mr Rane's words felt like daggers, and each one stabbed Rahul's heart.

'Dad, Mom, please stop it.' Karan pleaded.

'You stop it,' Rahul said in retaliation. 'It's because of you that I am getting to hear all this. So, don't try and act protective. I am so tired of hearing them say, "Karan did this" and "Karan did that". It's almost like I have no identity of my own. You may be good at academics but I am good at sports. Why should you be given preference over me? They won't accept me the way I am.'

Turning to face his parents, Rahul added, 'Just because I am average, I am a disgrace to this family. Do you even care about my likes and dislikes? Do you want to know why I didn't show you the remark I received? It was not because I was afraid of committing a mistake, but because I was afraid to face you after I'd committed it.'

Rahul left for his room, weeping hysterically. Karan tried calling after him.

'You can stop pretending now,' Rahul shouted back as he closed the door behind Karan.

Who was at fault? Rahul for the way he behaved or his parents whose attitude towards their child made him behave the way he did? Rahul was at fault for forging a signature, but what was more worrisome was why he had chosen to take that step. Rahul's parents should have just let him know that they were there for him and that grades did not determine whether or not he was a good person. This, however, they were far from doing.

~

Rahul was sandwiched between his parents' expectations and his own reality. This made him hate not only his parents but also his brother, Karan. At a tender age, if you're not made to feel wanted or loved, you develop perceptions about people whom you consider to be the reason for your suffering. And sometimes, these perceptions are hard to break.

'Rahul, where are you going at this hour? Wasn't your class cancelled?' his mother was curious.

'No, my class wasn't cancelled. Also, I have to submit some pending homework. Don't blame me if I don't, and this time, my tuition teacher calls you,' Rahul said wryly.

Rahul stood in front of the mirror debating what to wear. He finally decided to go with the black shirt he had got for his birthday. He preened himself, and after emptying an entire bottle of perfume, he left on his bicycle.

His tuition classes were on the right. He took the left instead. Karan saw Rahul taking the left, and because he was worried about Rahul, he decided to follow him. Karan followed Rahul's bicycle till he stopped outside a park. Since it was evening, the park was full of people and this made it difficult for Karan to locate Rahul. He caught sight of Rahul's black shirt and after a little walk, he saw him stop and sit on a bench facing the lake.

Karan knew that Rahul loved to go to the park with his parents, but he had never seen him go there alone. After many moments of inactivity, Karan noticed a girl walk towards Rahul and sit beside him on the bench. From the way they greeted each other, Karan sensed that they were more than friends.

Should I be sad because I am single or happy because my brother has a girlfriend? Damn! Isn't she gorgeous? I guess I might know who she is. Isn't she the one studying in the girls' school opposite to us? Oh, yes! Karan thought.

He had to admit his surprise. Rahul and a girl alone in the park, all by themselves, wasn't what Karan had been expecting. He felt a pang of jealousy rise up in him. He tried to conceal himself behind a tree in order to escape being noticed. But in his haste, he slipped on the wet grass and landed with a thud. The noise attracted

Rahul's attention and he looked at Karan, his eyes filled with horror.

Fuck! What am I supposed to do now? Should I run after Karan? But wouldn't that mean leaving Trisha alone? Why did you have to follow me, Karan, and ruin everything?

'What's wrong?' the girl sitting next to Rahul asked. Rahul was too astounded to speak. The girl shook his shoulders and repeated her question.

'Nothing. I have to go,' Rahul said, and rushed off, leaving the girl confused.

Rahul saw Karan fleeing on his bicycle and tried to stop him, but Karan sped away. Rahul immediately got on his bike and rode after him. The chase continued for a few minutes. Every few seconds, Rahul shouted Karan's name to make him stop, but Karan pretended not to hear him. The two finally stopped at a red traffic signal, side by side. 'Karan, please listen to me,' Rahul begged, and tried to reach for his hand but Karan dodged him. The fear was evident on Rahul's face because failing to placate Karan would mean another round of grilling at his house.

The moment the signal turned green, Karan accelerated to get away from Rahul. Rahul was getting irritated by Karan's behaviour. In anger, he crashed his bicycle's front tyre into Karan's back tyre. Since Rahul was conscious of his act, he balanced himself accordingly and sped ahead of Karan. He stopped his bike on the side of the road and waited for Karan to catch up. Soon after, he noticed a crowd gathering around someone who was injured. They were carrying the person towards the roadside. He was shocked to discover that the person being carried was Karan! Rahul jumped off his bicycle and ran towards the group of people who were still gathered around Karan. Pushing everyone away, he approached Karan who had passed out from the pain. A motorcyclist had run over Karan's leg after he'd slipped, probably from Rahul's act of hitting his bicycle's back tyre. The people helped admit Karan to the nearby hospital, and Rahul called his parents from the hospital's landline. He was too afraid to tell them the truth, so instead he only told them how Karan had slipped and been injured. Deep inside, he regretted what he had done. He knew very well that the consequences of his act could be far-reaching.

It's all my fault, Rahul thought, as he sat on the bench outside the room where Karan was being examined. *A few minutes ago, I was sitting on a bench in the park, and now, I am sitting on a bench in a hospital where my brother has been admitted because of me. I hurt him and I cannot forgive myself for that, even though my act was unintended. My insecurities about Karan and this constant pressure to keep up with him have made me a monster! Karan, please forgive me for being a bad brother to you. I am so ashamed of myself.*

Rahul felt awful about what had happened. He was guilty of an unintended crime and he did not know what would absolve him of it. Moreover, he was sure his parents would find out about his tryst with the girl, and they'd be even more ashamed of him. In the effort to get out of one mess, he kept getting into another.

His parents had arrived at the hospital and were asking him for the details of what had happened. Rahul was too ashamed to answer honestly, so he avoided explanations by describing it as a minor fall from the bicycle. Sometime later, the doctors appeared with Karan, who was in a wheelchair.

'It's an incomplete fracture. You can take him home, but just make sure that he takes rest for a minimum of three weeks and remember to bring him for a routine check-up.'

'Thank you, Doctor,' Mr Rane said gratefully. He pushed the wheelchair through the passage towards the exit. Mrs Rane could not control her tears when she saw her son in a wheelchair, but Karan tried to calm her down.

'What happened, Karan? How did you fall down and what were you doing there?' Rahul's mom asked with concern.

This time, Rahul was prepared for any scolding that came his way. If anyone was responsible for Karan's condition, it was Rahul. Had he not crashed his tyre against Karan's in a fit of rage, none of this would have happened. Although Rahul had only wanted to get Karan's attention, he had not foreseen the consequences in case Karan fell from being unbalanced.

'It's nothing, Mom. Rahul and I had gone cycling together. I tried to cross the road during the red signal and collided with a motorbike coming the other way.'

Rahul was dumbfounded by Karan's decision to save him from their parents' wrath. Karan had stayed silent about what had taken place in the park. Moreover, he'd forgiven Rahul for what he'd accidentally done to him. After they reached home, Rahul decided to speak to Karan, and perhaps to apologize. But his elder brother was too weak to talk.

~

When the world moves too fast and you are not able to catch up, you lose yourself in the chaos. That year, Rahul had been selected for the NCC, but his father considered it a waste of time and rejected the offer on his behalf. Rahul was one of the few students who'd been selected, and he tried hard to convince his family but they refused to understand. It did not make sense to them. Rahul's heart had splintered into pieces but he'd said nothing disrespectful. Karan was back on his feet, but he hadn't spoken with his parents about the unfortunate episode;

he also didn't open up with Rahul, who had tried to break the ice with him quite a few times. It was a Sunday, and having studied mathematics for almost an hour, Rahul closed his book and stretched a little. He got up and went to the kitchen, fixed himself something to eat and sat on the recliner to watch TV.

Karan was there too, watching *Mission Impossible*. Rahul liked the movie but was in no mood to watch it again. He tried taking the remote from Karan, but Karan held on to it.

'No, Rahul,' he said, his hands tightly clutching the remote.

'Don't you have to study?' Rahul said scornfully.

They continued arguing for some time till they heard their mother's shriek from inside her room. Her face was pale, indicating something terrible had happened. She was in a state of shock and could not find the words to speak. Mr Rane hurried to the bedroom to find stacks of files and folders sitting on top of the bed.

'What happened?'

'Somebody has stolen the envelope containing five thousand rupees. I am sure I'd kept the envelope in this drawer, and now it isn't here,' she said, pointing to a drawer of the almirah.

'Did you check the other drawers? Perhaps you moved the envelope and then forgot about it,' Mr Rane tried to pacify her.

'No, I had kept the maid's and the milkman's salaries in it. Today, I thought of paying the maid when she arrived in the evening but I can't find the envelope.'

'Nobody could have taken it. The maid only enters this room in our presence. Other than that, who's going to take it? I think you just need to check properly, Kavita,' Mr Rane tried to console her.

'Should we call the police, Dad?' Karan suggested.

Mr Rane continued, 'No! Don't be silly, Karan. The envelope must be around here somewhere.'

For the next couple of hours, Rahul's mother couldn't think of anything else and kept sobbing over it. Mr Rane tried to calm her down, but she was inconsolable. Karan was busy studying, but Rahul looked a little restless. His dad inquired why he was anxiously walking around in his room instead of watching TV or studying.

'What's wrong? I have been observing you for the past hour. Did you get a remark again at school?'

'No, Dad, I didn't.'

'Are you sure?' Mr Rane looked suspicious.

'Yes.'

'Then go and get your remark notebook. Let me see it for myself.'

'Trust me, Dad, there's nothing,' Rahul tried hard to convince his father, but to no effect.

With a heavy heart, he walked towards the corner where he'd kept his bag. Unzipping it, he retrieved his remark notebook and looked back to see his dad waiting impatiently.

'Bring it fast.'

'Why won't you trust me?' Rahul tried one last time.

'I just don't,' came the sardonic reply.

With trembling hands, Rahul handed over the notebook to his dad who took it from him. He sat in his chair and opened the notebook. Rahul rushed beside him, beads of sweat forming on his temples. The moment Mr Rane opened the notebook, Rahul closed his eyes with dread. Mr Rane pulled out a white envelope from the centre of the notebook. Mrs Rane gasped. The family was in a state of shock. Rahul may have been troublesome, but they couldn't have imagined him as a thief. Tears rolled down Rahul's face. What followed was no surprise to anyone. His father gave him a sound thrashing and scolded him for daring to do such a thing. His mother kept asking why he'd done it, but Rahul refused to break his silence. No matter how much he was scolded and beaten, he refused to utter a word.

'You have crossed all limits today. I am fed up with being answerable for your actions. Having a good-for-nothing child is better than having a thief for a child. Why don't you just leave the house and do as you please?' Mr Rane screamed at him in a fit of rage.

That night, Rahul left the house.

It's said, 'Family is where life begins and love never ends.' But Rahul had neither got the life nor the love he wanted from his family. The next morning, no one could find Rahul in the house. He had left, and all he took with him was a photograph of his family as a memento. He was about to journey into a new realm—a different world—leaving behind a letter in his remark notebook.

Mom, Dad, I am sorry once again. Sorry that I let you down one more time. I know it was hard raising me, and I know you both had your own ways. I don't blame either of you for anything; I just wish you could understand. I really wish you could. I wish I could have run into your bed on those nights and felt your arms around me. I wasn't a problematic child. I was a child with a problem. Mom, Dad, you didn't lose me today. You had already lost me the day you started comparing me with Karan. Dad, I wish I could tell you the reason behind me taking such a big step. I know you want an answer but I just can't give you one because I know you won't understand. I know I was wrong, but weren't you also wrong somewhere? Just ask yourself why this actually happened, and the answer will be right in front of your eyes.

Mom, I know you wanted me to be the best and I hope you know that I tried. It's just that I realized too late that trying to be the best was futile. Karan will always be better than me, but why should this reality upset me? I did not want to disappoint you, so I constantly cut off my edges trying to be the perfect circle you wanted me to be, but I'm far from it. I'm a square. I was trying to make you proud but I just can't do this any more—live this game of pretence. And because of your comparison, I could never share with Karan the bonding brothers have. I always thought of my elder brother as competition, but was I at fault? You may ask why I didn't tell you that I was sad and that all this had tormented me for so long. I did. I told you when I started shutting myself in my room. I told you when I said I wasn't hungry and stopped doing schoolwork. You simply dismissed me as lazy. I became more and more quiet. You didn't hear my silence because you weren't listening. I know that you love me and this knowledge has always kept me strong. I just wish you could step into my shoes for a day and study my situation from my eyes, understand my emotional outbursts, and my struggle to belong here—with you. I have decided to leave because I do not know a better way of getting rid of this misery. One day, I will be back and you will be proud of me.

Without thinking about the struggles and obstacles that he would face, Rahul walked on. Struggles are like washing machines—they twist, they spin and knock us around but, in the end, we come out cleaner, brighter and better than before. The day Rahul left his house, he was naive, vulnerable and impulsive. Years later, he returned as an intelligence officer. His profession spoke volumes about his character. And yet, his struggles, as we know them, were not over.

Chapter 4

'When is she coming? Akriti, is that correct?' Karan inquired.

Rahul nodded. 'She should be here in the next few minutes.'

After a pause, Rahul spoke, 'So, you knew why I'd taken the money?'

'Yes, your friend told me. I met him on the day you left the house,' Karan smiled knowingly.

'Do they know about it?'

'No. They don't know anything. Even the bicycle lie remains intact,' Karan winked.

After Karan left the room, Rahul switched back to the video call with Akriti. She had heard the entire conversation.

'You robbed money from your house?' Akriti asked, surprised.

'It's a long story that I'll tell you some other time. For now, I want you to concentrate on making a good impression on my parents. I'll hang up now. Come soon.'

Neither Akriti nor her parents were convinced that Rahul could persuade his parents to accept him, let alone accept their relationship. But things were happening for real in the Rane household. Rahul was nervous, not only because he didn't know if his parents would let Akriti stay at their house, but also because his brother's meeting with his in-laws had turned into a debacle, and he'd been the primary cause of it.

When Karan returned to Rahul's room, he could not stop himself from thanking his elder brother. 'Karan, thank you for saving my arse all the time.'

Karan laughed. Then he said, 'It's great to see you like this. The INA is a prestigious organization. I am really proud of what you have become.'

Rahul was touched by his words.

'I want to know the details of what happened after you ran away. How did you go about your life?' asked Karan.

'I will tell you the complete story someday. I remember that the initial days were really frightening,' Rahul replied softly.

'And what happened to the girl you were romancing in the park?' Karan teased.

'That was merely a childhood infatuation,' Rahul laughed.

Karan joined him. Once their laughter had subsided, Karan went and sat next to Rahul. He put an arm around Rahul's shoulder and said, 'Some stories of our childhood are best forgotten.' Rahul nodded.

~

The doorbell rang and Mrs Rane opened the door. On seeing Akriti, she smiled nervously. 'Hello Aunty,' Akriti greeted Rahul's mother.

Once everyone was seated in the living room, Mr Rane broke the silence, 'I heard the two of you intend to get married.'

Akriti blushed, 'If that's what Rahul has told you, Uncle.'

'Do you know love marriages are against our family principles?'

'I feel it is all right to replace old principles with newer ones in order to accommodate changing times,' Akriti was swift in responding. Her bluntness disturbed Mr Rane.

'How many years have you known each other?' Mrs Rane inquired, trying to avoid any heated arguments that she knew were par for the course in her family.

Mr Rane interrupted her, 'Your parents are okay with you seeing each other?'

'Yes, Uncle, they've known about us for a long time. They are in favour of our marriage and want us to get married soon. As a matter of fact, they are only waiting for your approval.'

'These days parents pretend to be as ignorant as their children,' Mr Rane pointed out to Mrs Rane, who was glancing at him nervously. Akriti switched the position of her legs in discomfort.

Rahul wanted to retaliate, but Karan stopped him.

'My parents wanted the approval of Rahul's parents before we got married,' Akriti said politely.

'Oh! So, that's why you're here, all of a sudden,' Mr Rane stared at Rahul accusingly.

'Dad, let's investigate the reason for me being here later. Can we please discuss the plans for our marriage first?' Rahul said, 'Without your permission, it is impossible to continue.'

Akriti added, 'My parents are very fond of Rahul. He used to stay as a paid guest at our house.'

'Paid guest? You mean Rahul stayed with you in your house?' Rahul's mom was stunned.

'Yes, Mom, but with her parents around. It's not like we were alone,' Rahul answered for Akriti.

'We've also been young, Rahul. We know how it is with youngsters. Don't try to teach us,' Rahul's father remarked.

'If you've also been young and done the same things, then simply give us permission and get this over and done with. Why create a fuss?' Rahul was upset.

That made Mr Rane lose his temper and he blurted out, 'What kind of permission do you need? It's not like you've done anything with our permission in the past. Who are we to stop you? You know very well that love marriages are not acceptable to us; she does not even look like she belongs to our caste. So don't expect things to be grand. We are not willing to face our community and be answerable for an irrational and unprincipled marriage.'

Rahul's mother tried to ease the atmosphere by asking Akriti to help her with serving snacks. She was not against their union but did not wish to give her consent in front of her husband. After all these years, she wanted to see her son happy, but she did not dare to oppose Rahul's father. She had learnt to live a compromised life.

After Akriti had left with Mrs Rane for the kitchen, Rahul spoke, 'I don't believe it. She is a freelance software developer, and here we are discussing her caste and community. You know what, Dad? Even if you people earn a million dollars, your thinking will still remain poor.'

Karan tried to calm him down.

Mr Rane got up and walked towards the window. He always did this when he didn't wish to look someone in the eye. Without looking back, he said, 'If you guys have already decided, it doesn't make sense to go against your decision. You can get married if you want to. Although we still don't approve of the match, we are ready to give our consent. We'll help get the formalities done but don't expect much from our side.'

If it were up to Rahul, he would never have asked for their consent. Because Akriti's family had been so persistent about receiving approval from Rahul's family, he had been left with no choice. Also, he had a bigger request pending.

Looking at his mother, who had appeared with a tray of snacks, Rahul said, 'Till our wedding, Akriti will stay with us. Her parents are out of town and I don't want her staying in a hotel.'

Rahul did not wish to reveal the real reason behind Akriti's stay. He didn't want his parents to be apprehensive about the danger that was lurking in Akriti's life. They would never agree to invite the danger upon themselves if they knew about it.

'I don't think there will be a problem with Akriti staying,' Mrs Rane tried to sound helpful.

'For fifteen years, this house had not seen a trace of him, and now he takes decisions as if he owned the place,' Mr Rane spoke to the air, before leaving for his room.

~

If something has to be created, something else has to be destroyed. Every creation comes with a cost. Even revamping comes at the cost of dust, and currently Rahul's house was covered with dust. Nothing was right, yet everything had the facade of being so; no one was absolutely right, yet everyone was right from their own perspective—everyone had their own explanations to give, their own stories to offer. Rahul knew the days ahead would be tough with both professional as well as personal issues to take care of. He also knew that Akriti would feel uncomfortable living in a different environment altogether, and that made him consider how a girl after marriage has to forgo everything related to her past to step into a new reality—someone else's reality.

Yet, it was unfathomable how Rahul had brought his family around to not only consent to their marriage, but to also let Akriti stay at their house. The cultural walls of the house were getting renovated, and Rahul was the architect.

The next morning, Akriti was helping Rahul's mother prepare breakfast.

'So, you are a freelancer? What does that mean?' Rahul's mother asked Akriti.

'I don't work for a particular company. I take projects from multiple companies and adjust my work timings accordingly. It kind of gives you your space as you are your own boss.'

'Good for your generation. You people are not stable in anything that you do. I hope you're stable with your marriages, at least. No freelancing, I suppose,' Rahul's mother tried to joke.

Akriti was appalled by her bad sense of humour.

'You're funny, Aunty,' she let it go.

'You can call me Mom,' Rahul's mother smiled and patted Akriti's back.

'Sure.'

'But anyhow, I won't be hearing that a lot from you since you and Rahul will leave as soon as you get married. I wouldn't even know how to stay in touch,' she frowned.

'Don't worry, Mom. I will call you regularly even if Rahul doesn't.'

'We'll see,' Mrs Rane concluded with distrust.

It was hard trying to adjust to Rahul's family. Mrs Rane tried to make conversation with Akriti but always ended up saying something hurtful. Mr Rane, on the other hand, didn't acknowledge Akriti's existence. Akriti did not wish to bother Rahul with her feelings of discomfort because she knew he felt as out of place as she did, if not more so. Rahul had returned to his family after fifteen years and a lot of things had altered since then. Except for traditions. Cruel and ugly traditions. So, Akriti tried, as hard as she could, to blend in with the family of her fiancé. Rahul had been right about his family. They weren't easy people. Rahul stayed away from his family but it didn't mean he hated them. He still loved them but his loyalty was questioned. Even after returning, he was looked down upon. Not all scars show, not all wounds heal. Breakfast was served. Karan was in a hurry to leave for work, so he declined to eat. Mr Rane and Rahul were seated at the table.

'The food looks delicious. Did you make it? Why don't you join us for breakfast?' Rahul asked Akriti.

'I made it. And you didn't care to ask me to join you for breakfast?' Rahul's mother replied sharply.

'The food is great, Mom. I suggest you both join us for breakfast,' Rahul tried to please her.

'No, we'd rather wait on you,' Mrs Rane was upset.

'I wanted to tell you people not to wait for us at dinner. Akriti and I are going out and might be late,' Rahul informed them.

'We've had dinner for a decade without you,' Mr Rane always knew what to say.

~

'Can I ask you something?' Akriti said, seated in the passenger seat of a car they had hired from Zoom car services. Rahul was driving on Matheran Road enjoying the fresh breeze. Akriti was holding his hand over the gear lever. He nodded and Akriti continued, 'Why did you steal money when you were a kid?'

'There's nothing really interesting about that story,' Rahul avoided revealing the truth.

'Why do your parents treat you like this? I mean, they behave well with Karan, but with you, they're almost always blunt.'

'Do you also think so? Maybe it's because I am adopted,' Rahul laughed.

'Shut up. I am serious,' Akriti glared at him.

'They want everyone to behave the way they like them to. Follow their standards, obey their rules. I happen to have a different ideology and they cannot swallow that. I love them, there's no doubt about that in my heart. But that does not give them the right to humiliate me.

50

My only problem is—if they seek respect, so do I. How difficult is that for them to understand?' Rahul said, with a tone of rebellion in his voice.

'Hey, let's talk about something else,' Akriti said, leaning towards Rahul as a romantic song began playing on the radio.

Their marriage was fixed for the weekend. They had decided to have a simple ceremony with the family, and they had informed Akriti's parents who were flying in the day before. Akriti sank back into her seat, relaxing as she opened the window. 'Old music never fails to create the right vibe,' she smiled. Her silky hair blew delicately in the breeze; her eyes closed and a tiny smile played on her lips. The last couple of days had been stressful for both of them. Rahul was happy they'd decided to go for a drive.

'How about a kiss right here in the middle of the road?' Rahul took his hand off the gear lever and rubbed it over her thighs. She was looking stunning in the outfit she wore—a knee-length dress which had risen, revealing her skin, as she sat.

'I think you should concentrate on your driving,' Akriti teased. 'I am very hungry,' she added.

'I am hungry as well. Allow me to eat you right here,' Rahul said, shifting his face towards Akriti.

'A burger is a better option,' she said, pointing at the food mall sign she'd spotted a few metres away.

'That's unfair. Should we book a hotel room and stay there overnight to make up for the loss of a kiss?' Rahul suggested playfully.

'No, Rahul,' Akriti replied with a smile, as Rahul halted the car on the side of the road.

Eventually settling for one peck on her cheek, he got out to buy a burger for her.

'At least, park the car inside. There are no cars parked here.'

'I'll quickly get you a burger. Till then, think about my plan,' Rahul winked and walked away.

Akriti checked the notifications on her phone before closing her eyes to take a nap. Rahul appeared a few minutes later carrying two burgers and a pack of fries. He walked towards the car parked on the other side of the road, hoping Akriti would at least consider his plan of spending the night in a hotel. He knew she wouldn't and he smiled, thinking about how stubborn she could sometimes be. He opened the door to the driver's seat. The window on the passenger's side was still open, allowing the cool breeze to waft into the car.

But there was no sign of Akriti. Rahul was numb and couldn't comprehend what had happened in the blink of an eye. He searched for Akriti all over the place but was unable to find her. Even the passers-by claimed they had not noticed anything unusual.

What had started as a romantic road trip had ended up becoming a terrifying nightmare. Rahul had stepped out of the vehicle to buy food for Akriti only to return to an empty car. Were the same people who tried to enter her house responsible for this act, or was it someone Rahul didn't know about? Too many questions popped up in Rahul's head—everything seemed to be in a maze—only one thing was clear: his fiancée was missing.

Chapter 5

Everything was lost in that brief moment. Rahul was sure he had not taken that long to return but here he was, looking at an empty car, registering the absence of his girlfriend. Rahul had searched the entire area including the food mall, hoping to find Akriti but in vain. Who'd taken her was no mystery to him. They must have been the same people who'd attacked her house the other day, the people who he suspected were on a bigger mission that somehow involved Akriti. What appalled him was his carelessness, his decision to leave Akriti alone in the car. He was an intelligence officer. How could he have made a mistake? He was accountable to Director Rajiv Jain for Akriti's safety, and he had failed miserably to perform his duty. He felt someone tap his shoulder and turned to look around, praying it was Akriti. It wasn't.

It was Rashi, the girl who'd come to see Karan the day before. Rahul was unable to understand her presence in the current scenario.

'What are you doing here?' Rahul asked her.

'I am here to help you,' Rashi announced.

'Pardon?' Rahul was confused.

'You heard it right. I am here for you. I work with the Research and Analysis Network (RAN) and I am here on a mission.'

'Do you know what you're saying? I am in no mood to take a joke.'

'Can we just take a seat inside so that I can clear things?'

Rahul couldn't understand what was happening. A minute ago, his girlfriend had disappeared into thin air, and now another girl whom he'd only met recently, in completely different circumstances, was telling him she worked with RAN. Rashi, without taking it further, showed him her identity card.

'I didn't know you were Karan's brother. I had researched everything about you and Akriti, but somehow I skipped that—probably because you had no connection with your past life. When I saw you at Karan's house, I was surprised. I couldn't even introduce myself as someone working with RAN. I have been tracking you guys since the attack at Akriti's house. The day that incident took place, RAN was alerted and since then I am on a mission to discover the motive behind it. We fear that there is a conspiracy involved. I followed you to Mumbai. A little while after you entered the food mall, I felt the need to use the restroom, and when I returned, Akriti was missing. My car was parked at a distance behind yours.'

She continued, 'Since the mission is feared to be a conspiracy, we decided not to disclose our involvement to the INA, which is why you don't know about me.'

'All right, I believe you,' Rahul said, at last.

'There's something else I need to tell you. I found a note on the seat where Akriti sat.'

'A note? What does it say?'

Rashi handed over the note to Rahul and he read it out loud—'I'm everywhere and nowhere. I own nothing and everything. Karma will return to you. I'm your past and I'm here to make you pay.'

'What does this mean?' Rahul flipped it over to see if anything else was written, but apart from that ridiculous riddle, it said nothing.

'What is it about your past that makes the person write this? Was there someone before Akriti came into your life?'

'I have no idea what this is all about.'

'Do as I say. First, inform your family that you will be late, and second, ask your friend who is waiting at the hotel to trace her location.'

'How do you know about Neerav?'

'I already told you, I am on a mission. Now tell me everything you can remember about your past relationships.'

'But why? Can't we just go and find Akriti instead?'

'Rahul, this is about a national threat and I request that you cooperate. Akriti is being used as a scapegoat, and if there's any chance of us finding her, it is through you.'

'National threat? Are you serious?'

'Yes, the nation is in danger and we have limited time.' Rahul stayed silent for a while before he began telling Rashi about his past. He would do anything to get Akriti back.

~

Eighteen years ago

Rahul was getting his uniform ready for school when Karan burst into his room to inform him that both Mom and Dad wanted to talk to him. Walking out of his room, he could hear faint whispering coming from the living room. His parents were talking to each other in hushed voices, but the second he walked into the room, they stopped. His mother turned to look at him with a wary expression; his father, on the other hand, looked like he wished to discuss business. His expressions were always indecipherable. 'Come, sit down,' his father told him in a gentle but firm voice. His mother looked a little embarrassed.

'What happened, Dad? What's the matter?' Rahul asked, eager but also afraid to know the truth.

'Dad had some work on his laptop but his CD was not getting detected,' Rahul's mother said.

'So?'

She signalled Mr Rane to speak and he did, 'So, I decided to use your desktop and the CD worked. However, before I could complete my work, I found something in your recycle bin.'

Mr Rane continued, 'It was a clip.'

'An HD clip,' Rahul's mother emphasized.

Holy shit! How could I forget to delete the clip from the recycle bin? Fuck! He must have seen the porn clip for sure. More than 20 GB carefully hidden in the hard disk, but one deleted clip screwed up everything.

'When I tracked the path of that file, it led me to a hidden folder. The folder was full of dirty films,' his father said gravely.

Porn, Rahul thought. *Why was it so difficult to call it porn?* Nevertheless, he was angry with himself for not making the videos less accessible. Now he was answerable to his parents, who, by the way, were always looking for reasons to needle him.

'Well, Karan has an entire hard disk dedicated to such videos. Lecture him first. I'd very much like it if the two of you compared us in these matters too,' Rahul said, unable to come up with a way to defend himself.

'This is serious, Rahul. We understand that you are growing up and, at your age, boys are curious. Still, we do not encourage this behaviour. I don't wish to see this kind of thing happening in the future. Otherwise, your desktop will no longer remain yours,' his father told him.

'At least then the child will open his books,' his mother frowned.

Rahul did not say anything in return. He simply went to his room, donned his school uniform and left for school.

On his way to school, he saw a girl on a Ladybird bicycle entering the school opposite his. With olive skin and honey-coloured eyes and hair the shade of chestnut brown, she was the prettiest girl he'd ever laid eyes on. He waited till she had entered, and then he pedalled his bicycle with a crimson face towards the parking lot. Her face, still so novel, flashed in front of his eyes until he met Sandy.

'You look quite happy today. It's not Friday yet.'

'I know. I just saw such a beautiful girl you would be mesmerized. I watched her enter her school gate. She was so innocent, yet so ravishing. I couldn't help imagining myself with her.'

'Is that so? What level did your imagination reach?' Sandy asked.

'Riding bicycles together; holding hands while walking on silent roads.'

'And?'

'And . . . nothing. Then all of a sudden, I remembered my dad seeing the porn clip on my computer,' Rahul declared dejectedly.

'What, your dad still watches porn? And that too on your computer?'

'No, idiot. That would've been fine by me. Instead, he accidentally saw the porn clip I had deleted after watching but had forgotten to erase from the recycle bin.'

Sandy could not stop laughing.

'What was their reaction?' Sandy asked, still laughing.

'I told them Karan had an entire hard disk full of those,' Rahul replied.

'You're kidding. Why don't you tell him to share some?' Sandy said gleefully.

'Shut up and show me your homework. I haven't completed it yet. I have to finish it before the lecture begins.'

Even while he was finishing his homework, her face flashed on the pages of his notebook—so clear that he could have touched her. For him, she was like a song whose tune he'd just heard, but would never forget for the rest of his life.

~

Every period in school seemed longer than it was, as if the minute and hour hands were in a conspiracy to not move that day. At last, when the bell for the last period rang, Rahul picked up his bag and rushed outside the classroom. Sandy ran behind him. He wished to see if the girl looked as beautiful as Rahul had described her to be.

'Are you sure you'll be able to recognize her? Since her school must have also just gotten out, it will be difficult to spot her in the crowd of students leaving for their homes,' Sandy showed concern.

'Don't worry. I can locate her in a crowd larger than this.'

Both of them ran outside their school building. Rahul stood in the exact place from where he'd seen her that morning. He anxiously waited for the girl to appear.

An hour passed but there was no sign of her.

'That must be her. Look, she is so hot,' Sandy exclaimed.

'Stop eyeing girls, dumb-ass, and let me concentrate,' Rahul kept glancing in every direction in the hope of finding her somewhere in the crowd.

'You could have been Albert Einstein if only you concentrated as much on your studies,' Sandy exclaimed.

'Stop trying to sound like my parents,' Rahul berated him.

'No, I'd never be like your parents. I'd never ask you to delete porn,' Sandy laughed.

'Why isn't she coming out?' Rahul was growing impatient.

'Because she sensed a moron was following her and left early,' Sandy teased.

'Are you trying to call me a moron?' Rahul looked angrily at him.

'I am not trying. I just called you one,' Sandy laughed again.

'If we were anywhere else, I would have beaten the shit out of you,' Rahul told him.

'Exactly! That's what I have been suggesting. We should be somewhere else instead of waiting here for your imaginary beauty,' Sandy replied.

They waited for another forty minutes but she was nowhere to be seen. 'Let's go, Rahul. She must have left school early,' Sandy declared, exasperated.

Rahul finally gave up and pedalled homeward with a long face. He kept thinking about her, wondering why she hadn't been in the crowd of leaving students. Could she have bunked classes to hang out with her friends?

Had she fallen ill and left for home early? He worried about the latter.

The next day, he followed his ritual and waited for her outside school but to no avail. He'd waited for so long that he'd arrived late for his first class. But this time, the teacher let him go without a remark for being late. Rahul decided that things were looking positive and he would somehow get to see her that day.

'Any success?' Sandy asked out of both concern and curiosity.

'Nothing yet. But I am confident I'll get to see her today,' Rahul answered. On his desk, he was scribbling his favourite romantic song.

After school ended, Rahul was back in his spot with a look of confidence in his eyes. Sandy preferred watching Sachin bat on the Wankhede pitch rather than accompanying his dreamy friend on a hopeless expedition. This time, Rahul didn't have to wait long to see her. There she was on her Ladybird bicycle coming out of the school gate. He quickly pedalled his bicycle to follow her. Moving behind her, he watched her hair fly from the sides that had escaped her ponytail. She halted her bicycle next to a stationery shop and Rahul followed suit. Parking his bicycle right next to hers, he walked inside the shop.

'Can I get a Parker pen? The red one,' she asked one of the attendants.

After the attendant had handed the pen to her, she began arguing over the prices of files and notebooks. This was the first time that Rahul had heard her speak. Her voice was as sweet as sugar, her pauses punctuating her breaths.

I am captivated by your voice; it's taking me to places I could have hardly imagined. It's not just your words but the beauty within that captivates me.

He was so lost in that moment that he did not notice her leave. It was only when the attendant spoke to him that Rahul realized she'd gone.

'Do you want something?' he said, raising his eyebrows. He first looked at Rahul and then in the direction where the girl had headed.

'Nothing. Thank you.'

The attendant shook his head scornfully as Rahul left in haste.

Rahul slowly caught up with the girl and when the signal turned red, their bikes stopped next to each other. Rahul looked at her from the corner of his eye, too afraid to talk to her. He'd been following her all this time but she pretended to take no notice. She looked straight ahead, impatient for the signal to turn green. He frowned at his inability to make the first move.

It wasn't until the signal went green that she turned to look at him and smiled for a brief moment, before disappearing in the chaos of the vehicles. He wished she could have stayed longer, not sure if he would see her again soon. There was every reason to blame the Mumbai traffic.

Chapter 6

Love is as peaceful as it is chaotic. Peaceful because it lends you a placid look in your eyes, as you scroll through romantic tunes resonating with your heartbeats. Chaotic because despite your calm disposition, thoughts are racing in your head; thoughts that rid you of your sleep; thoughts that cause you to daydream. Rahul was happy because this was the closest to love he'd ever been.

'Have you topped a class test? Why are you dancing like crazy?' Rahul's mother inquired.

'I just feel light today. As if I am free from the worries of the world. You only get one life, Mom. You should live it and you should love it. I have decided to explore the beauty of my life. Fall in it, swim in it and float in it. My English teacher was right: we should value relationships. I value you, Mom, I value Dad, and I value

Karan and everyone else. I value my schoolmates and even those who study in the school opposite to mine. We should love everyone. Isn't that true, Mom?' Rahul was blabbering dreamily.

'Yes, as of now, go and love your history book. You have a school test tomorrow,' his mother replied sharply.

Poor woman, he thought, *she does not understand love.*

Rahul couldn't stop thinking about her. He dreamed that she whispered in his ear and told him that she loved him. It felt so real that he thought he could hear her speak.

Every day, he'd wait for her before school, and then follow her after school till they reached the traffic signal, where the two headed in different directions. He did not follow her to her house. He kept waiting for her to turn and look at him and smile like she had done before, but she never did. He was too afraid to speak to her and this worried him. With time, it made him sad because he could not picture his love story moving any further than this.

Sitting in his room, he would gaze at the ceiling, lost in thought. Oh! How he prayed she'd acknowledge him, at least once.

Falling for her taught him how to value someone's presence, but he had no clue how to deal with someone's absence. His wish to meet her was fulfilled the next morning when he waited for her outside school. She was on her bicycle and was pedalling towards her school gate. He told himself he had to break his silence today. They had a long vacation ahead of them due to Ganesh Visarjan, which meant he wouldn't be able to see her until it ended. This was his only chance and he had to make the most of it. Without further thought, he shouted, 'Hello, the girl on the bicycle.' After ascertaining that she hadn't heard him, he shouted louder, 'I am talking to you, Ladybird girl.'

This time, the girl heard him and she turned to look at Rahul. In that moment, Rahul felt goosebumps on his skin. He was once again left speechless. Not knowing how to react, he stood there like a mannequin. On receiving no response from Rahul, she turned away and, without acknowledging him, she went inside the school gate, leaving Rahul dejected again. This was not the kind of encounter Rahul had hoped for.

Fate had a way of pulling them together, but it was up to Rahul to take the first step. And as of now, circumstances were evidently not on his side.

~

All he wanted from the world was her. Even a glance from her was enough to tickle his nerves. She, on the other hand, knew nothing about him. She wasn't even aware of the existence of her lover who would go to the world's end to do anything that made her happy. They say drowning is bad but he wanted to drown . . . in her love. He wanted to swim in the deepest parts of her soul and be pulled in— he wanted the currents to take him to places close to her heart, so he could feel her heartbeat surround him.

Love has made me a poet, Rahul thought. He could think about her all day long. Sometimes, she entertained his dreams. He did not wish to wait until after Ganesh Visarjan to see her again.

To his amazement, his next meeting with her was shortly after, as the festival brought with it a surprise for Rahul. Students from every school, who were good at extracurricular activities, were selected to volunteer for an environmental awareness event. Rahul was one of them. Miraculously for Rahul, his dream girl stood there, as a part of the rally, holding a placard for pollution control, along with all the other students. Rahul, who'd been mentally absent until then, jumped up in delight.

Ganpati Bappa Morya! chimed in his heart.

She stood a few students away from him, and he cautiously moved towards her. He tried to push his way through the students who, in turn, gave him annoyed glances. He did not care in the least, and soon he was standing a few inches from her. He stood silently, not knowing what to say. He saw her glancing towards him a couple of times and wondered if she recognized him from the other day when he'd called out to her.

'Hi. Are you from Holy Cross?' Rahul finally gathered the courage to speak.

'Sorry?' she turned towards him, pretending she hadn't heard him.

'I was asking if you studied at Holy Cross,' he repeated his question.

'Yes. Why? Do I know you?' she inquired. Her voice was playing with his senses again.

'I've heard about a teacher at your school who also offers home tuitions for mathematics. I've heard she teaches very well,' Rahul said. He'd learnt this piece of information from the frontbenchers at school.

'Yes, Miss Perera. I go to her classes after school.'

Well done, Rahul, he applauded himself.

'Does she teach boys as well?'

'Yes,' she smiled.

'Okay, thanks,' Rahul smiled back.

That was all Rahul needed to sustain him for the day. He did not try to talk to her after that. In his mind, he relished the idea of sitting next to her. He always knew that they were meant to be, and that God would find a way to bring them together. It was time Rahul concentrated on his weakest subject. The first step would be to take tuitions for mathematics.

~

It was one of the rare occasions when Rahul was confident about asking his parents' permission. Every demand of Rahul's was fulfilled after a lot of scrutiny, but when it came to his studies, his parents did not question him much. They were happy that their child wanted to join private classes to improve his mathematics. They happily handed over the fees to him, which he paid the next morning itself due to a free day at school. Miss Perera asked him to attend the afternoon session and, for obvious reasons, he looked forward to attending it. After having lunch at his house, he prepared to leave for class.

Surprises were a part of Rahul's life; he was always ready for them. He got a big surprise when he reached the society complex where Miss Perera taught. It turned out that Sandy also attended the same classes, and the moment they saw each other, Rahul kicked him on his calf.

'What are you doing here?' Rahul inquired.

'What are *you* doing here?' Sandy asked, surprised to see Rahul.

'My girl . . . she studies here.'

'Here? At Miss Perera's tuitions?'

'Yes, and you never bothered to tell me that you attended tuitions here or about the girl I love taking these classes with you,' Rahul said, annoyed.

'Wow. You want me to tell you about a girl although you haven't told me her name, her class or anything else.

All you knew was her school, and in this class, there are so many students from Holy Cross. How on earth was I supposed to know that your dream girl studied here?'

'All right, sorry. Let's go,' Rahul indicated that they should go upstairs.

'What's her name?' Sandy asked.

'I don't know.'

'What? Then how did you get to know she studied here?' Sandy was curious.

'Long story,' Rahul dismissed Sandy's curiosity.

Rahul located his girl sitting on the second to last bench. The class had just begun. Both Rahul and Sandy sat on the last bench, which surprisingly was vacant. Rahul was disappointed when he received neither a friendly greeting nor an acknowledging smile.

'Now, who's your girl?' Sandy asked.

Rahul pointed to where she was sitting and, in return, Sandy told him that she was his friend.

'Really?' Rahul couldn't believe his fortune. Sandy nodded. Rahul was a little relieved knowing that it would be easier to get himself introduced to her. An introduction was, after all, the first step where most relationships failed even before commencing.

'Why didn't she greet you then?' Rahul wanted to be certain.

'She is very serious in classes but equally fun outside. Her name is Trisha.'

Trisha. So, that was what his Ladybird girl was called. Her name was as enchanting as her personality. 'Trisha. Trisha. Trisha.' Rahul kept repeating her name under his breath. He loved the music it created on his lips. Once the class was over, she turned back to greet Sandy.

'Can you give me your notes of the last lecture? I couldn't attend the class for some personal reason,' she asked Sandy.

'Sure. You can take my notebook, but don't forget to bring it tomorrow. By the way, this is Rahul, my best friend at school.'

'Hi, Rahul,' Trisha greeted him.

'Hi, Trisha. How are you?' Rahul spoke.

'Oh! So you already know my name? Very nifty, I must say,' Trisha teased.

Rahul smiled shyly in response. Perhaps he should have considered asking her name. Sandy said, 'Rahul told me you guys have met before?'

'Yes,' Trisha replied, 'on the day of Ganesh Visarjan.'

The classroom was silent, except for them. Sandy looked around to realize that everyone else had left and Miss Perera was waiting for them to leave.

'Sorry, Miss, we were just leaving,' Sandy apologized, and the three of them hurried outside.

Once outside the complex, Sandy invited Trisha to join them for a quick round of pani puri.

'Not today. I have a lot of pending homework. You guys continue without me,' Trisha was about to leave when Rahul stopped her.

'Oh, come on! Just ten minutes won't do any harm.'

'Sorry, Rahul, I am quite particular about my homework.'

'And he is particular about you,' Sandy said softly.

'What?'

'Nothing. Let's catch up tomorrow,' Rahul finally spoke.

'Sure,' Trisha smiled and left.

Rahul kicked Sandy in the calf once again although he was more than grateful to his friend for introducing him to Trisha. Trisha agreed to a round of pani puri the next day, and Rahul said it was his treat. Rahul hardly tasted the pani puri as his concentration was exclusively on her. She was a beautiful distraction, and he couldn't believe his luck.

'Thank you for the treat, Rahul. You are really sweet.' Every word from Trisha was like a reward for Rahul. After their little adventure, Rahul kept gazing at Trisha as she walked away. He was happy that they had exchanged their landline numbers. Her style of walking—with swift steps so that her hair swirled as she walked—was insanely beautiful. She was everything he had ever wanted in a girl.

'Keep going, bhaiya. You are bound to get her, one day. I, too, loved a girl when I was your age,' said the loquacious pani puri vendor.

'Did you get her to love you?' Rahul asked, putting another pani puri in his mouth.

'No, she got me beaten up by her brothers,' he laughed. Rahul stopped smiling.

Unlike the pani puri vendor's love story, Rahul was not beaten by any of Trisha's brothers. Instead, his meetings with Trisha increased with time. Conversations on landlines were now prolonged and passionate. Like a love song in a movie, their romance bloomed quickly.

Chapter 7

One month later

Life isn't that hard; we make it hard. The sun rises and then it sets—we just tend to complicate the process. Rahul and Trisha's togetherness was special because they were too naive to understand the complexities of life—with no insecurities, no space for jealousy, their bond was pure and sweet ... Rahul and Trisha had decided on a secret code for communicating on the landline. They gave each other three brief missed calls before finally picking up on the fourth ring. This way they knew it was the other calling and could ensure that their parents did not pick up. In those days, when cell phones did not exist, this was a lifesaver.

That night, Trisha received three missed calls on her landline at half past twelve. She picked up on the fourth ring, anxious to talk to Rahul. No matter how often they spoke to each other, their conversations never seemed enough to them.

'Hello?' Rahul spoke on the other end, cautiously waiting to confirm it was Trisha.

'Have you looked at the time? My parents could have woken up from the noise of the phone ringing.'

'Thank God, it's you! I was reluctant to call at this hour, but I had something important to tell you,' Rahul said.

'Which is?' Trisha asked softly, afraid to wake up her parents.

'I called to ask if we could bunk our tuition tomorrow as there is nothing important that is going to be taught. Miss Perera will teach the basics of algebra, which you and I are both familiar with. I know you are particular about classes, but could you please at least consider it for me? Tomorrow marks the completion of a month of us being friends,' Rahul struggled with the word 'friends'.

'Of course, I didn't realize we'd been *friends* for a month,' Trisha said, emphasizing the word 'friends'.

Rahul stayed silent. He knew he'd have a reply to Trisha's remark tomorrow.

'So, where are we going?' Trisha asked, breaking the silence.

'I don't have a place in mind. I just wanted to spend some time with you,' Rahul lied.

'I am not bunking my class to go to a random hang-out spot,' Trisha replied, smiling inwardly but sounding stern.

'Okay, fine. It'll be some place special. In fact, I am taking you to my favourite hang-out spot,' Rahul assured her.

Trisha smiled and terminated the call. On any other occasion, Rahul would have called back to find out why Trisha had ended the call without a reply. But tonight, he knew she'd been too happy to respond. He knew it because he was so happy himself, so happy that he was sure he wouldn't sleep at all that night.

~

The next day, when Rahul was getting ready to go for class, his mother questioned him, 'Rahul, where are you going at this hour? Wasn't your class cancelled?'

'No, my class wasn't cancelled. Also, I have to submit some pending homework. Don't blame me if I don't, and this time, my tuition teacher calls you,' Rahul said wryly.

Rahul stood in front of the mirror debating what to wear. He finally decided to go with the black shirt he had got on his birthday. He preened himself and after emptying the entire bottle of perfume, he left on his bicycle.

His tuition classes were on the right. He took the left instead. He pedalled towards the park where he'd planned to meet Trisha. His feet pedalled with a joy he'd never experienced before. After parking his bike, he waited on a bench for Trisha. He'd given Trisha the address in the morning and she would be here any minute. One of the best things about Trisha was that she was punctual, unlike most other girls who made their boyfriends wait; although Trisha and Rahul had not started a relationship yet. The thought made Rahul blush. First love is such a pure and blissful experience that the world around us transforms into a happy place. Love is a whole gamut of emotions that race through your heart—the butterflies in your stomach and the train of timid thoughts in your head—almost as if every little thing is in a conspiracy to keep the redness of your cheeks alive. Both Rahul and Trisha didn't need 'I love you' to justify their bonding. In the last month, whatever time Rahul and Trisha had spent together, they had experienced a different dimension of life and they had come to love it.

Rahul sat on the bench facing the lake in the park where he had asked Trisha to meet him. He did not have to wait long for her to arrive.

Trisha came, wearing a bright blue dress that tapered at her waist and then flowed till her knees. As she sat next to him, he wished he could watch her without saying a word.

'So, it's been a month to our *friendship*, Rahul?' Trisha was incorrigible.

'To me, you're more than a friend. You're the only person who has made me feel that I am worth loving,' Rahul spoke softly.

'What about your parents?' she asked innocently.

'My parents? Not really. My parents have always treated me like I was good for nothing. I am sure they won't even allow me to join the NCC. All they're worried about is my schoolwork so that I can get a job in a good company.'

'You got selected for the NCC and they wouldn't allow it?'

Rahul nodded. After a pregnant silence, Rahul spoke, 'So, I was saying that you make me feel special. And I want to thank you for that, Trisha.'

Rahul leaned closer to Trisha and kissed her on her cheek. She looked down shyly, not knowing what to do.

'Am I allowed to do that?' Rahul asked.

She smiled and nodded softly.

Rahul kissed her cheek again. She could sense his lips moving towards hers, so she withdrew nervously. Her hands felt clammy and her cheeks were on fire.

But he seemed anxious to feel her lips against his. He wrapped his arms around her waist, pulled her towards him and gently touched his lips against hers. This time, she let him and they kissed for a while before she pulled away.

'My first kiss,' Rahul beamed and Trisha smiled nervously.

That was my first too and it was beautiful, Trisha said to herself.

They sat in silence together. Trisha rested her head against his shoulder. This was turning out to be the best day of Rahul's life, until he heard the sound of someone falling on the ground. He was shocked to see his elder brother, Karan, who'd probably slipped on the grass. As soon as Karan understood that he'd been noticed, he picked himself up from the ground and hurried towards his bicycle. Trisha could not understand what was happening. All she knew was that Rahul looked shocked to see someone.

After Rahul regained his senses, he spoke, 'I am really sorry, Trisha, but I'll have to leave right away.'

'Who was that?'

'My elder brother, Karan. I am really sorry but I have to run. Bye.'

He apologized to Trisha for leaving and rushed towards Karan, who was already out of the park. The chase on the bicycles intensified until they stopped at the red signal, but it became serious when Rahul intentionally crashed his cycle into Karan's. Rahul balanced himself and cycled forward, but a motorcycle ran over Karan's leg after he'd slipped. Karan was admitted to the hospital immediately. Rahul felt responsible for the entire incident. Karan, who had a fractured leg, didn't reveal anything to their parents. Rahul had left Trisha in haste and severely injured his brother.

Some days start beautiful and end ugly, Rahul thought. Trisha was embarrassed about the whole incident. Rahul's elder brother had caught them kissing, and she could not bring herself to talk to Rahul. While Karan had almost recovered after a week, Rahul's love life failed to recover even days later.

~

'Trisha, listen to me, at least. You aren't even giving me a chance to speak,' Rahul was walking behind Trisha, after class, trying to talk to her.

Trisha turned around to face Rahul, folded her arms and said, 'What do you want to talk about?'

'What happened was not my fault. Why are you behaving like this?'

'Rahul, I am not saying that any of it was your fault. It's just that I don't feel like talking right now. Leave me alone for some time. Also, can you please stop calling me on my landline? My parents are getting suspicious of the blank calls. Before long, they'll put a caller ID on it.'

Trisha had a tone of detachment in her voice. Trisha's silence was suffocating Rahul, especially because he could not understand what he had done wrong. He dreaded losing the only person who believed in him. He couldn't eat because eating had become a mere act of swallowing. He either slept for a full day or did not sleep at all. He tried talking to Trisha multiple times, but she always gave him the same indifferent response and walked away. Sandy tried to help by talking to Trisha but his attempts to resolve their tiff also failed. Even after three weeks, she was adamant about her decision to keep her distance.

'Why don't you write her a letter? She doesn't want to talk, but at least she can read what you have to say. I will hand it over to her,' Sandy suggested, and since Rahul knew no other way of reaching out to her, he decided to give it a try. He prayed that it would work.

Love can make a person do things he would never have contemplated doing before. A boy who couldn't write an essay for an English examination was writing an apology letter to woo his beloved. Rahul tried to pen his thoughts on a piece of paper. He tried to express what he'd always felt for Trisha. At times, he would imagine her response after reading a line he'd written. By the time he was finished, he was sure the letter would convince her of his feelings. He handed the letter to Sandy. Sandy, in turn, gave it to Trisha who showed little interest as she threw the envelope in her bag and left.

After reaching home, she locked her room and retrieved the letter from the bag with a smile playing on her lips. Her plan had worked. She had wanted Rahul to express his feelings for her, and she knew that the only way to get him to speak was to pretend that she was upset. She giggled, although a part of her felt bad for worrying him for such a long time. It is true when people say that it is impossible to read what's going on in a girl's mind. She slowly began to read the letter.

I can't tell you how sorry I am for what happened. I didn't know that the most beautiful moment I'd shared with a girl would be destroyed in a jiffy. Karan had a fractured leg because of me; he is still recovering. I am sorry for leaving you alone like that. Will you forgive me one last time, Trisha? Life is a scary place without you by my side. Let's put one bad incident behind us and carry the warmth of each other's presence forward. Will you be my girlfriend? Please take your time to reply and remember that I love you . . .

Trisha had tears in her eyes. Once she was done reading, she gave Rahul three brief missed calls on his landline. Rahul, who'd been waiting by the phone all day, jumped up in excitement. He waited for the fourth ring with his heart pounding in his chest. When the phone rang again, he picked it up immediately.

'Let's meet somewhere and talk,' Trisha said promptly.

'Did you read the letter?'

'Of course I did. That's why I called you. Let's meet on Monday after school. Will you buy me a gift to apologize?' Trisha smiled.

'Thank you for calling, Trisha. You don't know how happy you've made me. Let's meet at the same place in the park on Monday. No more troubles, I promise. And yes, I will get you the cutest gift.'

'Okay, then. See you on Monday,' Trisha said, 'and one more thing, Rahul?'

'Yes, Trisha?'

'I love you too,' Trisha hurriedly cut the phone.

Rahul couldn't stop smiling for the rest of the day. He wanted to buy something special for Trisha, but that month, he had forgotten to ask for his pocket money. Since Monday was only a day away, and on Sunday most markets were closed, he had to purchase the gift by tonight. He ran to his mother's room to ask her for some pocket money, but when he got there, he remembered that she'd gone shopping. He was about to leave disappointed when he noticed an envelope sticking out of a drawer. He opened it to discover a bundle of cash inside it. Rahul only needed some of it. He decided to take the required amount and leave the rest. Then, after purchasing a gift for Trisha, he would ask his mother for his pocket money, which he could use to replace the money in the envelope. This way, he would have done nothing wrong. He was about to take some of the cash when his mother announced her arrival in the drawing room. Afraid, Rahul quickly took the envelope with all the cash to his room. He kept it in his remark notebook that he kept in his bag and went downstairs to greet his mom. He prayed that his mother wouldn't need the money soon. Later in the day, he purchased a small gift from a gift shop near his house. In his excitement, he forgot to put the envelope back in the drawer.

On Sunday morning after studying for an hour, he got up and went to the kitchen, fixed himself something to eat and sat on the recliner to watch TV, where he fought with Karan about which movie to watch. Suddenly, they heard their mother shout from her room and everyone rushed to find all the files and folders scattered on the bed.

'Somebody has stolen the envelope containing five thousand rupees. I am sure I'd kept the envelope in this drawer, and now it isn't here,' his mother said, pointing to a drawer of the almirah. She was clearly distressed. The colour drained from Rahul's face.

Mr Rane asked her to remember where she'd kept it, but she was sure she'd put it in the drawer. For the next couple of hours, Rahul's mother couldn't think of anything else and kept sobbing over it. Mr Rane tried to placate her, but to no effect. Karan was busy studying but Rahul became a little restless. He started anxiously pacing about his room.

'What's wrong? I have been observing you for the past hour. Did you get a remark again at school?' Rahul's father inquired. When Rahul shook his head, he was ordered to get his remark notebook. Rahul tried to convince his father that nothing of the sort had happened, but failed. With a heavy heart, he walked towards the corner of his bedroom where he had kept his bag. Unzipping it, he retrieved his remark notebook. He wanted to conceal the envelope elsewhere but his father was standing behind him, with his eyes glued on Rahul. He finally handed the notebook to his father.

When his father discovered the missing envelope between the pages of the notebook, Rahul was thrashed severely. In his anger, his father ordered him to leave the house and that really upset Rahul. He cried for hours, locked inside his room. In the evening, he called Sandy and narrated the entire episode, still trying to control his tears.

'Rahul, will you follow my suggestion?' Sandy said.

Rahul stayed silent.

'I think it's best that you leave. Your parents will never accept you for who you are. So, live life the way you want to live. You don't have to tell anyone—not even me—about where you are going. Just prove to your family that you're not a failure.'

Rahul was too defeated to object to a voice that sounded reasonable. He could not find a reason to stay either. An immature mind was giving life advice, ignorant of the world outside, and another immature mind was captivated by the idea. Rahul wrote a letter to his parents before packing a few essentials in his backpack and leaving the house. As he was leaving, he thought of his mom, his dad, Karan and Sandy. But he mostly thought of Trisha and how disappointed she would be when she didn't find Rahul in the park. This was definitely not the surprise he'd hoped to give her.

He had to erase people from his memory. The toughest face to forget would be Trisha's, the girl on the Ladybird bicycle and, even as his eyes welled up with tears, the memory of her face made him smile wistfully.

Chapter 8

Present day
Highway cafe

'So, you did not meet Trisha again?' asked Rashi, who'd been listening to the entire story intently.

'Never, but before leaving, I left the gift at the place where we had decided to meet,' Rahul confessed.

'I am sorry to say this, Rahul, but you behaved rather immaturely, leaving your house on a silly suggestion from a friend, and then after all that, you didn't bother to meet Trisha—leaving her clueless about what could have happened to you,' Rashi stated.

'I don't want to dwell on what happened in the past. All I can say is that had I met Trisha, it would have been impossible for me to leave. She was my only weakness

91

and my sole reason to stay back. To avoid that situation, I simply decided to leave without informing her,' Rahul said pensively. Then, suddenly remembering his current predicament, he added, 'The only reason I decided to tell you about it was because you considered the knowledge of my past important in order to be able to find Akriti.' It had been hours since Akriti had gone missing.

'What about your friend, Sandy? Where is he now?' Rashi asked.

'I have no idea. We didn't contact each other after that day. Without mobile phones, it was impossible to stay in touch.'

Rashi was tracing circles on the table with the tip of her index finger, lost in thought. Rahul was plagued with thoughts of Akriti. He'd hoped his story would help them find her, but looking at Rashi's deadpan face, his hope was slowly disappearing.

'What's the matter?' Rahul finally asked.

'I don't know whether you'll believe what I am about to say next,' Rashi replied.

'Go on, tell me,' Rahul was more worried than curious.

'How many years have you and Akriti been together?'

'It's been a while now. A year, maybe. What's the matter?' Rahul asked, sounding puzzled.

'A year is not long enough to know much about your girlfriend,' Rashi speculated.

'What are you trying to say?' Rahul's curiosity had heightened.

'Officer Rahul, we suspect that your girlfriend, Akriti, is a spy,' Rashi declared. 'She was here to steal confidential information from the INA, which is why she pretended to be your girlfriend for a year,' she continued.

Rahul's jaw dropped upon hearing this. Then he felt his anger rise. 'Are you out of your mind? I am not going to put up with baseless allegations against Akriti,' he said.

'Officer Rahul, I request you not to be guided by your emotions. The RAN has sufficient proof that Akriti is a national threat. Since Akriti was transferring confidential information from the INA, we were ordered to not disclose our involvement in the mission to the INA,' Rashi tried to make Rahul understand.

'You're saying that Akriti helped organize an attack in her own house? Or was the RAN involved in this, as well?' Rahul said scornfully.

'No. RAN was not involved in the attack. There is no doubt that somebody wants Akriti murdered. Probably because of the information she is carrying. We were spying on Akriti even on the day the attack took place. We were about to catch the assailants and interrogate them about Akriti and what they wanted from her, when you and your friend arrived on the scene and we had to abandon our plan. The INA team is good for nothing but upsetting the apple cart. You people interrupted an effective plan. The government should take note that the RAN is better at handling critical operations than the INA,' Rashi spoke with derision.

'Are you trying to create a power struggle between RAN and INA? The government need not take note as they know who's better than whom. Also, we are not here to discuss who's superior. A girl goes missing in broad daylight, and all you're concerned about is who is better handling missions. If RAN can handle critical situations, why are you incapable of doing anything after hours of knowing that she is missing?'

'All we are doing is clearing up the mess your team has created, as always,' Rashi said, trying to avoid Rahul's question. 'Anyway, I think your girlfriend has either fled out of fear of being suspected or she has been held captive by the assailants. I have already informed the team and they've put all the exit points on alert,' Rashi continued.

'Pretty story,' Rahul exclaimed, 'but do you have the proof against my girlfriend with you now?'

Rashi shook her head, 'Unfortunately not. But I can bring some evidence tomorrow if that will convince you of the legitimacy of my accusations.'

'Then I guess we'll meet tomorrow. You have my number,' Rahul said, getting up to leave, 'and if your allegations against my girlfriend turn out to be false, Officer Rashi, you'll be sorry for this.'

Rahul left the building with several thoughts racing through his head. He was trying to convince himself that Akriti was being framed for a crime she did not commit. In the time he'd come to know her and love her, he'd never once suspected there was anything wrong. She had never shown such signs, and how could she bluff an intelligence officer? He wanted to be convinced of her innocence, but her absence was disturbing. He wished there was a way he could find her. Then, he was reminded of the confidence with which Rashi had spoken about Akriti's identity and a number of questions began forming in his head. *What was the information that Akriti had wanted to get hold of? Where was she from and what were her intentions? Who had wanted to attack her in her house? Did she really choose Rahul as her target? How was his past related to her recent disappearance? What information had Rashi obtained to prove that Akriti was a spy? Who was the missing link that she was trying to find, and did she truly believe that his past would help them find Akriti?*

In this gamut of uncertainties, Rahul knew only one thing for certain: if Akriti was a spy, as Rashi had alleged, he could never proudly call himself an intelligence officer again.

~

On his way back to Mumbai, Rahul called Neerav to inform him about everything Rashi had told him. Neerav expressed the same shock Rahul had.

'How's that possible? I can't imagine Akriti is a spy even in my wildest dreams.'

'I can't either, but she seemed so sure about it,' Rahul said.

'Do you trust this girl, Rashi?'

'I don't know. She said she would bring proof tomorrow to turn her allegations into claims. She'd suggested calling you and asking you to track Akriti's location. Did you find anything?'

'The team is working on it. They'll share the details with us soon. Didn't you find anyone suspicious on the scene where Akriti went missing?'

'No such person. I interrogated several people but they knew nothing. Anyway, I am returning to Mumbai. I'll meet you once I get there,' Rahul said.

'Sure,' Neerav replied.

As he rolled down the windows, Rahul took out a cigarette and lit it as he drove on the national highway. The music was turned off so he could feel the whistling sound of the breeze as the speedometer touched a hundred. Cold tears ran down his face. He stared at the road ahead of him; his helplessness distressed him. All of a sudden, the sound of a continuous beep caught his attention. At first, it felt so distant he thought he was hallucinating, but the sound did not die down. He closed the windows to get a better idea of where the sound was coming from. He checked that all the doors were shut properly. But that beep was unfamiliar and did not stop. He looked at the back seat of the car but found nothing. It was only when he opened the glove compartment that the intensity of the sound increased. After rifling through a couple of diaries, he finally located the source of the sound.

Inside the glove compartment was a time bomb on which the timer blinked seven minutes. Rahul had seven minutes to save his life!

First Akriti and now me. This seems to be a planned attack. Who could be behind all this planning? Could Akriti be involved? he shook the thoughts away.

Not knowing what to do, Rahul immediately dialled Rashi's number.

'You are early, Rahul. I can only get the evidence tomorrow,' Rashi said.

'Rashi, listen to me. There is a bomb in my car. Can you hear me? It's a time bomb that will explode in the next six and a half minutes.'

'What! This must have been Akriti's doing.'

Rahul was afraid to admit that the thought had occurred to him as well.

'The best thing to do right now is to leave your car in some isolated area and run. Just do that, Rahul.'

Rahul disconnected the call and took a sharp left off the highway on to the barren land around it. His car bumped on the uneven surface but he did not lower the speed. Once he'd found a suitable area, he stopped the car, opened the door and started running away from the car.

Boom!

After a couple of minutes, the car exploded and he turned to see it going up in flames. He was shell-shocked but breathed a sigh of relief as he thought of his narrow escape. He kept staring at the car, and as soon as a crowd began forming around the site of the accident, he informed the INA about it, so that the accident did not become news. The incident made Rahul wonder whether the INA had been right in trying to protect Akriti, or was it the RAN that was right in trying to trace her true identity?

~

The next day, Rahul's misgivings were put to an end when Rashi showed both Rahul and Neerav Akriti's original passport.

'I hope you got your answer, Mr Rahul. This is a Pakistani passport,' Rashi said, handing them the passport.

Both Rahul and Neerav examined it carefully. The passport contained her original name. *Afsana Nabi*. They could not trust their eyes. Rashi had proved that Akriti's only motive was to leak information, and marrying Rahul was not on her agenda.

'I don't know what to say,' Rahul said gravely. Neerav called the team to try and find out Akriti's location, but her it was changing continuously and they needed more time to get accurate information.

'You have to say something. First, everything that is happening is somehow linked with your past, and second, Akriti aka Afsana is not your lover but a spy. Now, what's the link that connects your past with Akriti's disappearance? The questions that remain unanswered are: Who planted the bomb in your car, and who tried to attack Akriti in her house? Were they the same people? When Akriti was here to leak information, she could have easily done that by marrying you, but she fled before the ceremony. Why would she do that? Or if she didn't flee and has been taken captive, then who is behind this? Was she here working as a developer to decode some information that only you could access? She could have achieved the same outcome by marrying you, but I think we are missing the link that connects your past with your present. The story is hidden there.'

'I still can't believe what is happening,' Rahul was perplexed.

'Mr Rahul, are you still defending her? Are you refusing to believe that a spy can easily pretend to be your girlfriend to deceive you?' Rashi said sternly.

When Rahul didn't say anything, Rashi spoke to him, 'Let's go over the details of your past again, Rahul. Let's talk about how you met Akriti.'

'I don't know how my story with Trisha helped you and I don't know how this will help either. Trust me. I did not suspect a thing when I was with her. I even stayed at her place as a paid guest,' Rahul told Rashi.

'Look, Rahul, while there's still time before your team responds with the information about Akriti's location and we are all idle here, why don't you enlighten us?' Rashi smiled cunningly.

Rahul could not think of any other way to find out what had really happened to Akriti. He knew Rashi was as clever as she looked, and he had little choice but to submit to her requests. She had brought everything that was needed to prove Akriti's guilt. He, on the other hand, did not know who to believe: the woman who sat facing him and had just shown him evidence of Akriti's deceit, or his heart, which still insisted that Akriti might be innocent. He looked at Neerav, who also looked helpless and signalled Rahul to proceed. Rahul's life had come to a point where he might have to choose between his nation and his love. He had never, in his wildest dreams, imagined this could happen to him. He loved his nation ardently, but he couldn't bring himself to deny the fact that he equally loved Akriti.

Akriti, what have you done? Have you really played me like a puppet all this time to get what you wanted? Did you never feel anything towards me? Were you playing a charade all this time? Could you have gone to the extent of planting a bomb in order to get me killed? Our moments—the ones we spent in each other's embrace—did they mean nothing to you? Are you really somebody else altogether?

Rahul was afraid to know the answers to these questions.

Chapter 9

Sometimes we know things we aren't glad to have known,
We see things that aren't meant to be seen,
Sometimes things aren't what they seem.

Sometimes we need someone to call our own,
Especially in times when we're alone,
To fill the absence of someone gone.

We did not know it hurt until we met pain,
Sometimes the hard thing and the right thing are the
same.

When you leave the comfort of your home for an unknown destination, the journey is unending and overwhelming. Rahul knew that it wouldn't be easy to survive without a family, but existence was different from surviving. Many people did not survive; they simply existed without a purpose.

Without his education, he was just a fourteen-year-old lad who could be hired either as a labourer or as a delivery boy. He did both simultaneously to make ends meet. He would attempt to throw newspapers in the balconies of houses, but more often than not, they would end up in the gutters and he would slap his head. Most nights he was hungry when he went to sleep, and he considered returning home but he knew he would not be welcome.

His parents did try to search for him for some time; they even lodged a complaint, but missing children were not found that easily. After months of searching, there was no trace of Rahul. His mother was worried to death; she kept regretting her misunderstanding with Rahul. She blamed herself for his absence. If only she could see Rahul again, she would beg for forgiveness and ask him to return. Eventually, his family lost all hope of ever finding him again. Rahul washed dishes in dingy restaurants on anonymous lanes, and from the meagre payment he received, he would eat his food in those very restaurants—in different utensils, of course.

Every morning he would wonder what kept him going and as each day passed, he realized he'd spent too much time away from home to consider returning. His meagre income kept him away from school for the most part. However, life had taught him what school could not have. One day, when he was working as a labourer in an ice cream factory, the owner took notice of him. Despite his worn-out pants and patched shirt, he still looked like he didn't belong there. The owner approached him and said, 'How long have you been working here?'

'I work on a daily basis, sir. When I can't find work elsewhere, I help here. The manager pays me accordingly,' Rahul answered politely.

'Don't you go to school?'

'My parents are too poor to afford schooling, sir,' Rahul lied. The owner was a Gujarati businessman and a careless lie was not enough to convince him.

'You seem to be from a good family. Did you run away from home?'

Rahul's face lost its colour. He was too scared to return to his family, who would still be spewing with rage. He could live the rest of his life doing menial jobs, but he could not imagine being handed over to his family. In response to the owner's question, Rahul vehemently shook his head.

'You can tell me the truth, son,' the owner coaxed him. Sensing Rahul's discomfort, he made him sit in his cabin and offered him an ice cream, which Rahul politely refused.

There was kindness in the owner's eyes that made Rahul believe he could confide in him. Something about his behaviour indicated that he was not curious but concerned. When Rahul had told him his story, the owner expressed sorrow over his situation. He suggested that Rahul return to his worried family, but Rahul refused to go back. Taking pity, the owner offered to take Rahul to his house. Rahul did not take his words seriously. It was only when the owner brought him to his house and introduced Rahul as a brother to his son, Neerav, that Rahul believed him. Rahul began attending the same school as Neerav and sat in the same class, although he was a few years older than Neerav. With time, Rahul and Neerav became best friends, and when Rahul missed his family, it was Neerav who consoled him. Whenever Rahul felt down in the dumps, Neerav would tell him, 'There are phases when we feel unsure and lost, but uncertainty is a part of everyone's life So, don't avoid it. Instead, take a deep breath and move forward. Soon, things will get better. Things are bound to get better. You'll be okay even if you don't feel okay now. It's okay to not feel happy all the time, Rahul.'

At times, Rahul would marvel at Neerav's kindness. Then looking at his father, the Gujarati businessman who'd decided to adopt him, he knew where it came from. Each night he thanked God for the gift of a new family. After completing school, both Rahul and Neerav shifted to Delhi, where they studied at the university in different colleges. In due course, both Rahul and Neerav had cleared their Grade II examination and completed their training as intelligence officers.

'Papa, Ma, if there is God on earth, it has to be you. I don't have enough words to thank you. My whole life wouldn't be enough to express my gratitude. When I was in school, I was selected for the NCC but my father did not allow me to go. He must have had his reasons and it is not my place to judge his decision, but my dreams had remained unfulfilled all these years until I met you. Today, after becoming an intelligence officer, I can lead the life I have always wanted to live, and this is all owing to your kindness. You happily took my struggles as your own, and accepted me for the undisciplined boy I was. I am so blessed to have parents like you and a supportive brother like Neerav,' Rahul said with tears in his eyes, on the day he'd earned his qualification. He hugged them and sought their blessings. That day he also missed his real family. He wished they knew about his achievement. How proud would they be! Every struggle in Rahul's life had shaped him into the person he was, and he thanked the hard times that had made him stronger.

Later that day, as they were travelling on their first mission, Rahul tried to tease his brother, Neerav, who'd also become an intelligence officer.

'So, what's your take on marriage—love marriage or arranged marriage?' Rahul asked casually to pass time during the tiresome train journey.

'Getting a girl itself is a task; marriage is, by far, the last stop on this train. We cleared our college from Delhi University and still stayed single. Do you think we can ever find a girl who would be suitable for us?' Neerav grinned.

'That's also true. But I think we will. Maybe we will meet someone during our training,' Rahul winked.

'Rahul, on a serious note, would you go back to your parents in Mumbai before getting married, whenever that may be?' Neerav spoke after recollecting a thought that they had discussed some time back.

'So, you still remember, right?'

'Yes, I remember you telling me once that you would want to at least go and meet them in order to seek their blessings,' Neerav smiled.

'To be honest, Neerav, I haven't really thought about it. I was so young when I left that life behind. But sometimes. I think I should at least visit them. However, I am not sure. I don't know whether they will accept me or not, and how would I justify the years I went missing? Such thoughts prevent me from going back. No doubt I still miss them, but there are many people in your life that you miss but can't be with. Aren't there?'

'So, you remember that was the thing I'd told you when we were young, in order to help you move on from your school love. What was her name? Trisha, right?' Neerav was impressed with Rahul for having remembered his words.

'Yes.'

'Lucky you. At least, you have stories. And here I am, in my mid-twenties, still waiting for my first kiss to happen,' Neerav made a joke about himself, and Rahul couldn't control his laughter.

A wave of nostalgia swept over Rahul. Trisha was the chapter of his life that had been the most difficult to forget. She had been his one true love and also his first. In his early days of struggle, he would often remember her smile. It would make him want to run back to her and see it for real. In order to avoid that, he had decided to completely efface her from his memory, as difficult as that had been. He had had no option but to move on.

~

A few months later, Rahul and Neerav had emerged successfully from many critical missions. They had solved the most difficult cases with relative ease. Rahul was known for solving critical cases with a calm demeanour, and Neerav was praised for his efficiency. One of their missions was based in Chandigarh. The duo took a train from Hazrat Nizamuddin. They were curious because they had been given no prior information about the mission. On reaching Chandigarh, Director Rajiv Jain welcomed them in a secluded building that had been transformed into a temporary office, and without wasting much time, informed them about the mission.

'Boys, you are in Chandigarh for a high-profile operation. "Tusk" has been handed over to the INA, and since you are two of the best officers, I want you to take charge of it.'

'Sure, sir,' Neerav responded.

'What makes "Tusk" even more important is the intensity of it. Reputations and integrity are at stake. Sources have revealed slight evidence of RAN's parallel participation in the mission. It does not matter to the ministry of defence whether they get their information from INA or RAN; all they're bothered about are the results. But for us, it is a matter of pride, so we have to deliver our best. Is that clear?'

'Yes, sir,' Rahul replied.

'The aim of "Tusk" is to get hold of a spy from Pakistan. The man is in India and is believed to be seeing the daughter of Major Tanna, who resides in Chandigarh. Rahul, I want you to confirm the identity of the target and keep an eye on all his activities, as well as the people he meets and interacts with. Neerav, you will monitor "Tusk" and take care of any needs that may arise during the execution. Our mission is not just to get hold of the man, but also to understand the depth of his intentions,' the director explained.

'How do I get access to the man?' Rahul asked.

'You will stay as a paid guest at Major Tanna's house. The major has put up an advertisement for the same, and we have already arranged your arrival by submitting your documents. Since his daughter is seeing our target, I suggest it would be easier if you gained access to him through her. Take care not to reveal your identity to the major or his family.'

'Don't worry, sir. We will catch the spy in no time,' assured Rahul.

'Any questions?' the director asked.

'What's the name of Major Tanna's daughter, sir?' Rahul asked.

'Akriti Tanna,' he informed them and added, 'These are the mobile phones and numbers that you would use. All the best.'

'That would be all, sir,' Rahul said.

Both Rahul and Neerav thanked the director and took their leave.

'Not fair! You are getting to stay close to a girl while I get to work behind the scenes. Your first interaction with a girl other than your childhood crush, isn't it?' Neerav laughed when they were alone.

'Doesn't matter,' Rahul replied seriously.

'The daughter of a major and an intelligence officer is quite a match. What if you end up liking her?' Neerav teased.

'That, my friend,' said Rahul, 'is a rare possibility.'

~

Sudeep Nagarkar

The next morning, Rahul, along with his belongings, reached the address given to him by the director. Every house on the street looked similar. When he finally reached a building with a matching house number, he was surprised to see no nameplate next to it. He looked around to see if he could confirm the address, but there was no one on the street except for a few vendors selling fruit and vegetables. Then he noticed someone on the terrace of the house and shouted, 'Excuse me?'

The girl turned to look down at him but said nothing.

'Is this Mr Tanna's house? Number 512?' he asked.

'No,' the girl replied.

'But it's written 512 here,' Rahul checked the number again on the wall beside the entrance.

'Then why are you asking?' the girl said and left, leaving Rahul dazed. Rahul assumed this was Akriti. In no time, a middle-aged woman opened the door.

'Are you looking for someone?' she asked.

'Yes, is this Mr Tanna's house? I am Rahul,' he said, adjusting the weight of his bag on his shoulder.

'Yes . . . yes, you are the guy who was interested in the PG offer? You spoke to me on the telephone, right?' Mrs Tanna inquired.

Rahul replied in the affirmative. 'I hope your journey was fine?' Mrs Tanna asked.

'Absolutely, Aunty.'

Mrs Tanna welcomed him inside and showed him his room on the top floor of the two-storey house they lived in. After they had finished the formalities and Rahul had handed over the rent for the first month, Mrs Tanna asked him to come down to eat after freshening up.

'And also remember the rules of the house—no girls, no liquor. If you are found with any one of these, don't make excuses; simply leave the house. Got it?' Mrs Tanna gave orders like the wife of an army major.

'Yes, Aunty. Don't worry. I don't drink.'

Mrs Tanna left and after unpacking his luggage and freshening up, Rahul went to take a look at the terrace. Akriti was seated on the terrace, reading a book. Rahul noticed how beautiful she looked even from a distance, her auburn hair glistening in the sunlight. He tried to shake his thoughts away and walked to where Akriti was sitting. 'Hi, I am Rahul,' he introduced himself to her.

'So?' she glanced up from the book she was reading to take a look at him.

'So, what's your name?' Rahul asked, despite her nonchalance. She did not respond and continued reading her book, indifferent to his presence. 'At least you can tell me your name,' Rahul said.

'Akriti,' she said without looking up.

'See, it wasn't that difficult, Akriti,' Rahul said, moving back towards the staircase.

'Whatever,' Akriti shouted back.

~

That night after dinner, Rahul went to the terrace for some fresh air. He was standing by the scaffolding when he heard Akriti shouting at someone on the phone. She had a beer in one hand and her phone in the other. She was seated in a corner so Rahul hadn't noticed her when he came. The moment he saw her, he couldn't help but stare. She looked ravishing in a black top and denim shorts. He was consciously pushing his feelings away, knowing he was on a mission.

'Do you know that you are the son of an ass? No, I'm not insulting you; I'm just describing you. Your ancestors must be cacti, because you're a prick. Trust me, if I had a face like yours, I'd sue my parents. Your birth certificate is an apology letter from the condom factory.'

Rahul was as intrigued as he was amused on hearing Akriti speak under the spell of alcohol, although he doubted if she was any different in her sober state. He preferred to wait until the conversation ended rather than interrupt her.

'How dare you cheat on me? I am going to make your life hell. I was so blinded by love that I agreed to get into a relationship with a shithead like you. You're so ugly that if your parents had dropped you at school, they would have been fined for throwing garbage. Now when I look back, I think I should have flushed you down the toilet because that's where you deserve to be. I wish there was some vaccine against people like you—you ugly disease, you are like a fucking Monday. No one likes you.'

She paused for a moment before starting again, 'Of course I am speaking like a lunatic, otherwise how would you understand me? Now, get lost and don't you dare call me again.'

She disconnected the call and looked behind to see Rahul standing there. Furious, she asked, 'What the hell are you doing here?'

'I ran out of fingers trying to count the insults you hurled at your boyfriend,' Rahul mocked her.

'Ex-boyfriend, we broke up yesterday,' Akriti corrected him.

'Of course. Why were you shouting at him, if I may ask?' Rahul said, taking the beer from her.

'If you were eavesdropping, you would have heard the reason. That bastard dared to cheat on me. From the beginning, my friends and family knew the shithole was up to no good, and they had warned me, time and again. However, every single time I brought up my concerns to him, he pushed them away and said that he loved me more than anyone could. That bastard! He swore his loyalty to me on every occasion. Until yesterday, when I found him with someone else,' Akriti fumed.

Rahul nodded sympathetically.

'And on top of that, he had the guts to invite me to a party tomorrow!' Akriti continued.

'So, why don't you attend the party with another guy just to make him feel jealous? That would be very vindictive,' Rahul suggested.

'Who'll go out with me?' she said in a dejected tone.

'That's for you to find out,' Rahul said.

He was about to leave when Akriti stopped him, 'How about you come along with me?'

'Me? Are you sure? You're too drunk to be taken seriously,' Rahul was taken aback.

'Come on, you are handsome. I want my ex to die of jealousy,' Akriti had a hint of naughtiness in her eyes.

'Okay, so where do we have to go and at what time?'

'The party is at Cottage Cafe at 7.30 p.m. tomorrow,' Akriti informed him.

After she had left, Rahul dialled a number and spoke into the phone, 'I am meeting the target at a party tomorrow. I will send you the location.'

This spy, thanks to Lady Drama, would be an easy catch, Rahul thought.

~

Rahul had insisted that they reach the cafe at 7.30 p.m. After much opposition from Akriti, who insisted the party wouldn't start before 8.30 p.m., they finally agreed to arrive at the cafe at 8 p.m.

'Where's your boyfriend?' Rahul asked looking around.

'He isn't here yet. If he were here, we'd know. He is a loud drinker. I'm telling you that guy is so dumb, he thinks Cheerios are doughnut seeds,' Akriti laughed as they sat at the bar counter taking their pints.

'Why were you dating such a guy in the first place?' Rahul asked, his eyes fixed on the entrance.

'Maybe because I wanted to improve my sense of humour by abusing that doughnut head?' Akriti laughed, 'Cheers!'

'Cheers to your break-up,' Rahul raised his glass.

'Do you have a girlfriend?' Akriti asked curiously.

'Are you hitting on me?' Rahul tried to sound playful.

'No. I am curious. I am sure you have one,' Akriti slowly picked up the bottle and touched it to her lips in anticipation of his answer.

'One is an understatement.'

'Oh, I like that,' Akriti sealed her lips, nodding her head.

'I am joking. I am single,' Rahul told her.

'May I ask why?'

'Well, that's a tough question. Probably because I could not find someone like you,' Rahul told her.

The atmosphere between them was warming up, and Akriti was enjoying Rahul's company. 'Partners aren't supposed to be like each other.'

'So how did he ask you out for your first date?'

'You won't believe this. He decided to read a letter to me on the phone before asking me out on a date. When he dialled and someone picked up the phone, he had read half the letter without knowing who was on the other end. It was my father, and after he got annoyed with listening to the long ballad he had written for me, he finally told the dumbhead I was not at home. And then there was a military parade at our house, and he came there—my father asked me to date someone with brains. But I thought it was cute of him and ignored his shortcomings. When we started a relationship, I was extra cautious to not let my father know,' Akriti told Rahul and both of them laughed. When their laughter subsided, they stared into each other's eyes until a man interrupted them.

While they were sailing on this ship of intimacy, their Titanic sank as the iceberg stood right in front of them—Akriti's ex-boyfriend.

'Akriti, I thought you weren't coming. Who is this guy?' the man, who Rahul assumed was Akriti's ex-boyfriend, inquired.

'He is my boyfriend,' Akriti said, placing her hand on top of Rahul's.

Her ex-boyfriend looked sternly at Rahul who immediately said, 'Dude, she is kidding. I am just a friend.'

'You don't need to be afraid of him, Rahul. He and I have broken up,' Akriti assured Rahul.

'No . . . no. I am Akriti's friend. She invited me over to the party,' Rahul defended himself.

'If he is your friend, how come I've never seen him before?' her ex-boyfriend turned to ask Akriti.

'Have I seen all your friends before? You didn't even introduce me to a close friend of yours before I caught the two of you making out. At least, I am courteous enough to introduce you,' Akriti said disdainfully.

'Anyway, we're having an after-party at my house tonight. You can bring this new friend of yours along,' he said before leaving.

'Thanks, man,' Rahul shouted back.

'What were you doing?' Akriti stared angrily at Rahul.

'You want to screw him, right? Trust me, let's go to his after-party and then leave everything to me,' Rahul told her.

'What if you try to back off again this time?' Akriti looked hurt.

'I won't,' Rahul promised.

Once the party was over, they left for the after-party at her ex-boyfriend's place.

'Your house is so dirty, I might have to wipe my feet before going outside,' Akriti rolled her eyes at her ex-boyfriend.

'Chill, babe. Enjoy your drink,' her boyfriend said, coming close to hold Akriti's waist.

'Dude, back off,' Rahul pushed him away.

Before anyone knew what had happened, a brawl developed. The two men were hitting and kicking each other on the stomach and face. Akriti was shouting for Rahul to break her ex-boyfriend's face. A few minutes later, Rahul's phone rang and, freeing himself from the blows of his opponent, he went to open the door.

The intelligence team was standing outside. Neerav, along with the others, entered and called off the party. A few men surrounded Akriti's boyfriend, which scared Akriti.

'Chill, Rahul. Leave him alone. That was more than enough. He's learnt his lesson.'

'Not yet. He is a spy and we're here to arrest him,' Rahul told her.

Akriti was shocked beyond belief.

Neerav dragged him outside, and Rahul went to his room to search for his documents. Once the locker was broken open, all his documents were sealed and his identity was confirmed. His real name was Rashid Nabi, and he was a spy from Pakistan.

'Thank you, Miss Akriti. You made our job easier by giving me access to the party to make your boyfriend jealous. We had expected it to take much longer but that was really quick,' Rahul thanked Akriti.

'And who are you exactly?' Akriti sounded confused.

'I am Intelligence Officer Rahul Rane. I had to stay undercover at your father's house to catch your boyfriend who is actually a spy and here to steal confidential information about the Indian Army that your father, Major Tanna, possesses,' Rahul explained.

'Wow! I can't believe I was dating a spy,' Akriti was stunned.

'They are trained to be undercover,' Rahul told her, 'just like we are.' He smiled and Akriti smiled back.

'I am sorry I had to keep my identity hidden. It's part of our duty. I hope you understand, being the daughter of an army officer,' Rahul said.

Akriti nodded. They stood silently for a moment. The chill in the air forced her to put her arms around her chest.

'So, Neerav is your colleague?'

'No, he is like my brother. His parents raised me. I'll tell you sometime.'

Should I tell him that I like him? But what will he think of me—that this girl is so modern, she switches boyfriends like shopping sites, whichever offers more discounts? No, I think I should let him do the talking. Was the bonding we shared also fake and part of your operation? Her eyes revealed what she wanted to ask.

I have begun to fall in love with you. Is there an easier way of telling you this? his eyes replied to what she wanted to hear.

They'd confessed everything other than the affection they had developed for each other. It was lingering in the air between them, waiting to be put into words. 'One more thing,' Rahul said.

'Yes?' said Akriti, half expecting Rahul to tell her that he liked her.

'For a few days, I'll continue to stay at your house so that no one suspects that Rashid has been arrested. Also, till the external factors are clear and I get a green signal from Neerav, my identity must remain hidden from your parents. Is that okay?'

'Yes, sir,' Akriti saluted him in a friendly manner and laughed.

Would she have the same response if I asked her to marry me? Rahul wondered. The thought made him smile.

Chapter 10

Have you ever come across someone you think about night and day—someone who can melt your heart with her presence? Have you ever met someone so special that you can no longer imagine your future without that person? Someone so crazy she can reduce you to laughter with her humour, and yet someone so vital she helps to keep you sane. Someone so beautiful that you wish you could pause time so a moment with her would not be lost to it. That someone for me is you, Akriti. Will you please be my girlfriend?

Rahul had made up his mind to send this message to Akriti. The more time he spent with Akriti, the more Rahul grew to like her. He knew Akriti, too, loved his company but she never dared to admit it. In the days that Rahul spent in Akriti's house, he had shone in her parents' eyes. They were impressed by the way he respected and treated his elders. His sometimes quiet and sometimes playful demeanour impressed everybody. That morning, he was talking to Mrs Tanna as she cooked food in the kitchen.

'Aunty, shouldn't you be thinking about Akriti's marriage now?' Rahul asked playfully.

'I have left that responsibility to the major. If the man can take responsibility for the entire nation and fight on the border, he can definitely take the headache of his daughter's marriage and convince her to marry,' Mrs Tanna told him.

'If you ask me, fighting the enemy on the border is much easier than fighting your daughter,' Rahul laughed.

'I know, Rahul. The last time her father found a suitable match for her, she declared she had a boyfriend. Now, only a few days ago, she told me that she'd broken up with that boy,' Akriti's mom said in a disapproving tone.

Both Rahul and Mrs Tanna were discussing Akriti, when she returned from the office.

'What's cooking?' she asked, peeping into the kitchen.

'As of now, *you*,' Rahul mocked.

'So, I was the topic of your discussion. I am sure it must have been about my marriage,' Akriti said wryly.

'How come you are early today?' her mom questioned as she went upstairs.

'I will have to leave again, Mom. I'll be home late as I have to meet a few clients to discuss the design of some new software,' Akriti replied.

After some time, Rahul bid goodbye to Mrs Tanna too. He had to attend to some urgent work. Once they were together outside, Akriti said, 'Did she suspect us?'

'I can't say. She is your mother. You'll know better,' Rahul replied.

Rahul and Akriti had planned to go to a movie, and so Akriti had come home from work early. Rahul had wanted to send her the message before she reached home, but owing to his reluctance, it remained in his drafts. They reached the multiplex in Elante Mall to find out that the tickets for the movie they had intended to watch had sold out.

'That's why I told you to book the tickets in the morning, but you preferred to gossip with my mother in the kitchen,' Akriti grumbled.

'Don't worry, let's watch some other movie,' Rahul tried to calm her.

'The movie starred my favourite actor, Salman Khan. Why would I go to watch any other movie?' Akriti said angrily.

'So that we can whisper in the movie theatre and have a great time,' Rahul smiled.

Akriti blushed and Rahul booked tickets to another movie that was streaming. There was time before the movie started, so Akriti inquired about Rahul's family.

Rahul's smile turned into a frown. Briefly, he told her about his family. He mentioned Neerav and his kind father and how they'd helped him to achieve his ambitions. Akriti placed her hand in his to comfort him. When the movie started, the two stole glances at each other, enjoying each other's presence. Rahul leaned in to whisper into Akriti's ear, 'You can remove your hand now. It's getting clammy.'

Akriti opened her mouth to object, but Rahul pulled her close and gently touched his lips against hers. Soon, they were kissing—his tongue exploring the corners of her mouth, his hand holding her waist as her hands grazed his back. Needless to say, they did not see much of the movie.

After they had returned from the movie and were in their own rooms, Akriti texted Rahul:

I keep falling in love with jerks. Am I falling for one again?

Rahul had smiled when he read the message and replied.

No, this one cannot cheat on you. He wants to hold your clammy hands for the rest of his life.

Akriti texted back:

There is no doubt that my love is yours alone because you were there for me when I was broken inside. You showed up in my life and the exultation in my heart knew no boundaries. Every moment we share together is special and dear to me. You have filled the void in my life— you have given me the half of myself that was missing. I must admit, you are the most amazing companion I could dream of having. Will you fulfil my deepest wish? Will you with all your heart and ardour propose to me? ☺

Rahul replied:

I've never had so much in my life to be thankful for. That was until I met you. I'd never believed myself to be worthy of someone's love. I was so immersed in my work that I'd forgotten that love existed. But with your sweet charm (and irresistible beauty, of course), you taught me how to love. Tomorrow I will fulfil your humble wish and make you feel as special as you make me feel.

~

It is not being in love that makes you happy. It is the person that you are in love with that does. Rahul and Akriti looked great together. Akriti had brought a new hope to Rahul's life, a hope that it wasn't impossible to find love again. For Akriti, it was Rahul who kept her sane at times when she wanted to explode.

That morning, Rahul got up later than usual and went downstairs to have his breakfast. As promised, he had made up his mind to express his feelings and fulfil Akriti's wish. He noticed some people sitting with Mr and Mrs Tanna in the drawing room. He did not wish to disturb them so he decided to go to the terrace to look for Akriti instead. A little nervous to open his heart in front of her, he made his way upstairs reluctantly. He knew she'd be there; however, he didn't expect her to be looking so gorgeous at this time of the day. She was wearing a pink Punjabi salwar kameez and her hair was tied in a bun with strands let loose from the sides. *If only I could get up to this sight each day of my life*, he thought. He walked up to her, looked into her eyes and pulled her towards him by her waist. Before he could speak, she broke the silence, 'Dad's friend's family is downstairs. They are here to discuss my marriage.'

Rahul was too baffled to speak. The emotional clamour inside him made his mind unstable. After he had registered the situation, he said, 'What the . . . just go and tell your father you don't want to get married right now.'

'And what excuse should I make? That I like someone, again? Who is that someone? What does he do? Can I tell him all of that, Intelligence Officer? No, right,' Akriti said wryly. Rahul stayed quiet because he didn't have an answer to Akriti's questions. 'Do something before it's too late, Rahul,' Akriti walked away, leaving Rahul all by himself.

Minutes later, Rahul called Director Jain to ask him how many more days he had to remain undercover.

'It's just a matter of a few days. Perhaps less than a week. Also, I would like to tell you that the ministry has applauded us for our success in this operation. Moreover, RAN failed to accomplish it before us, and their team has taken it as an insult. I am proud of you and the entire team.'

The INA had cracked the case before RAN and left RAN to mourn its failure. All those from the RAN that were associated with this operation had taken it as an insult and had planned to come back strongly to regain their pride. This battle of superiority did not affect Rahul because he had a tougher predicament to deal with. He did not wish his love story to end before it had even started. After speaking with the director, Rahul went downstairs to check the progress of the meeting. The look on Mr Tanna's face and the manner in which Mrs Tanna distributed sweets made it evident that Akriti's marriage had been fixed. Rahul looked at Akriti's fiancé clad in a suit two sizes larger than his size. When Akriti's fiancé smiled at Rahul, Rahul shook his head and left for his room.

Later that night, when Akriti and Rahul were sitting on the terrace, Akriti spoke softly, 'I'll get married if you just stay quiet. Please understand. Because of your mission, our lives will have to part ways.'

'Akriti, you have to understand. I cannot just reveal my identity and betray my duties. I had a word with my director, and he has confirmed that it's only a matter of a few days now. Can you stay strong until then?' Rahul pleaded.

'Can you stay strong through my marriage?' Akriti said and, once again, left him all by himself.

His heart was caught in a conflict. Bound by his duty to his nation, his hands were tied and his mouth sealed, while love escaped through the windows of his heart. With all his efforts, he wanted to keep his love alive, but his sense of duty debilitated him.

~

With each passing day, the tension between Rahul and Akriti was increasing. His relationship with Akriti was at stake, and though Rahul was well aware of it, he could do nothing but wait for the confirmation from the director.

'I don't want to watch a movie, Rahul,' Akriti told him. They were sitting on Akriti's bed, and Rahul was trying to lighten her mood.

'Then what do you want to do?' Rahul kissed her on her cheeks.

'You know there's something that I want *you* to do,' Akriti replied sharply.

'And I will do whatever you say. All you have to do is wait,' Rahul said, pecking her on her cheeks again.

'My parents have gone to decide a suitable date for my marriage. Are you even serious about us or is it all just part of your undercover operation? I have started doubting your authenticity now. When are you going to open up? Probably when I have kids, right?'

'I can give you kids right now,' Rahul moved closer to her, pretending to be calm and relaxed.

'Shut up, Rahul. I am serious.'

'I am also serious. Look at yourself—you look deadly in those shorts. I cannot take my eyes off you,' Rahul checked her out from head to toe.

'Why can't you understand? I don't want to lose you. I am afraid the way things are turning out, I will eventually. Please don't make me suffer like this. You know I can't love anybody else. Please . . .'

'Sshh . . .' Rahul calmed her down by putting his finger on her lips.

As they lay on the bed staring into each other's eyes, every second brought them closer.

'You don't understand . . .' she tried again, only to be interrupted for a second time.

She hated it when he avoided important conversation. *Why doesn't he listen to me? Does he think it's that easy?* she thought.

'Stay away from me,' Akriti moved a few inches farther away.

'Not possible,' Rahul said, moving closer to her. He put his arms around her and kissed her on her lips, 'I am not moving one inch away from here.'

Akriti started crying softly. He slowly pulled away and wiped a falling tear from her face gently with his thumb. She looked back at him and smiled weakly, 'I'm sorry, I do trust you. I love you.'

He didn't say a word, just pulled her closer, wrapping his arms around her.

He kissed her neck softly and began to move his lips lower.

'Rahul . . .' Akriti hesitated, but before she could say anything, he was undressing her. He was pulling up her top and unzipping her jeans. He began kissing her on her neck, then slowly moved down to kiss her belly. He laid her down on the bed, and then he took off his own shirt. Once he was on top of her, he traced her belly with his finger and kissed her on her neck and lips. He listened to her as she moaned. 'Rahul . . . please stop,' she managed to say, but he continued to kiss her. Akriti gave up and began kissing him passionately. She ran her fingers through his hair and curled her legs around his waist. The tenderness was reciprocated by Rahul and he could feel the dampness of her love. Like dew on the playing field, her skin flickered and the sprinklers splashed making the grass look greener. In their haste to exhibit their love for each other, they had forgotten to latch the door behind them. When Mrs Tanna opened the door without a knock, she shrieked with embarrassment. Both Rahul and Akriti were abruptly woken up from their illusion. They hurriedly put on their clothes and Akriti rushed outside the room.

When Rahul came downstairs and confronted Major Tanna and his wife, he was ordered to leave the house with his belongings.

He was too embarrassed to object or defend himself, so he packed his bag and left quietly. Even then he did not disclose his identity or try to woo her parents by professing his love for Akriti.

Akriti pleaded with her parents to forgive them, but the major's command could not be overruled.

~

'I miss you so much,' Akriti told Rahul over the phone, 'please come back or at least take me with you. Life is pure drudgery without you. I'll even go to a stupid movie with you.'

Rahul laughed softly, 'It'll all be okay soon. I promise.'

Akriti hardly left her room any more. She rarely went out for work, eating very little and sleeping a lot. Dejected, she wanted to reveal the truth of Rahul's identity but somehow held herself back. Mr Tanna could understand his daughter's misery and had told her that the only problem he had with Rahul was that he didn't know anything about his family or what the boy did for a living.

'This is about his family. Where are they and why are they silent? We can't just allow things to proceed without an assurance from them.'

Before Akriti could answer, the sound of a fork banging on a plate caused them to turn to face her mother. 'After all, it's your happiness that matters to us the most, but for that we have to make sure you are in the right hands.'

Akriti walked towards her room on the upper floor and slammed the door. She leaned against it and closed her eyes. Her face was pale with exhaustion and fatigue. She turned to place her ear against the door. Her parents were still arguing. These days, they were always arguing and most of the time, she was the subject. As she walked towards the bed, she thought she heard a noise above her head. It sounded like footsteps on her roof leading to her parents' bedroom.

She froze, not moving until the sounds were farther away from her. She took a deep breath, switched off the lights and quickly walked to her parents' bedroom where they were still arguing behind their own closed door. She raised a hand to knock, when all of a sudden, she heard the sound of breaking glass, her mother's screams and a gunshot. Tears sprang into her eyes as she registered what had taken place.

'Find the girl,' a deep, muffled voice ordered.

Frightened, Akriti rushed to her room once more, closing the door quietly and looking around frantically for a place to hide. She contemplated hiding under the bed but went into her closet instead, closing her eyes and hoping for a miracle. A few minutes passed and she let out a breath, relaxing in the darkness and trying to make sense of the events that had just taken place. She reached for the doorknob, when suddenly, it was yanked open and she stood staring at two men holding handguns. As the men realized who they were pointing their guns at, they relaxed and lowered them. Stepping back, they stood looking at each other.

When Akriti realized the men were Rahul and his friend Neerav, she instantly hugged Rahul.

'There is nothing to worry about. Your parents are okay. However, we couldn't catch the guys. I am sure they were associated with the same mission. Neerav was keeping an eye on your house, so we were able to get here in time.'

'Why are they trying to kill me?' Akriti asked.

'You'll have to come with us. Only you. Not your parents,' Rahul ordered, ignoring her question. Her parents, who were now standing safely next to Akriti, stared at each other with blank expressions.

'What's happening and where are you taking her?' Akriti's dad was worried. There were so many questions he did not know the answers to.

'Mr Tanna,' Rahul said, addressing Akriti's father, 'we are from the INA and I was at your house as an undercover agent.' Rahul narrated the entire story behind his staying at their house—how they had arrested the spy from Pakistan, and how he'd slowly fallen in love with Akriti but he could not reveal his identity until ordered.

'I hope you understand, sir. The man was a national threat and was here to leak confidential information that you possessed,' Rahul concluded.

Mr Tanna nodded while his wife was too shocked to speak. 'We are very proud of you, Rahul,' Mr Tanna said finally. Mrs Tanna couldn't hold back her tears. They had been so close to danger. Rahul sat beside her and consoled her, 'Aunty, everything is fine. Nothing will happen to any of you. Yes, I faked my identity in the interest of the nation, but when it comes to Akriti, I love her and that's certainly not fake. You know it; you are a mother and you have seen it in her eyes. Mr Tanna also loves his daughter more than anything, and I have seen it; his anger reflected his love for her. We are sorry for what you had to see but we plan to marry. I know you will take the right decision for your daughter and I leave it to you.'

Rahul got up facing Akriti, 'Remember you had asked me to propose to you in a special way? I couldn't think of a better way than proposing to your parents. Because if they are with us, no one can be against us. I am sorry for hurting you too, Akriti.'

Neerav smiled as his best friend and brother professed his love. Then he reminded Rahul that they had to leave.

'We will be taking Akriti with us in order to ensure her safety. We believe there's a motive behind her attack, sir,' Rahul explained.

'I understand,' the major said, 'but do you promise to take good care of her?'

'I won't let her out of my sight,' Rahul promised.

It's said if you love someone, let them go. But Rahul didn't agree with that saying. Because if you love someone, you should instinctively hold on to them, cherish them and never let go. Sometimes situations

Sudeep Nagarkar

may arise that make leaving a more comfortable option, a more convenient option. But by doing so, you may foolishly let go of the person you loved so much that they leave—temporarily, or perhaps permanently. Why would you want to risk that? Rahul was not ready to risk Akriti for anything. He had expressed his ardent love for her. Now, he would protect her with all his might. He had taken an oath, and as an intelligence officer and lover, he would do everything in his ability to fulfil it.

Chapter 11

'And then Akriti's father happily agreed to your marriage,' Rashi assumed.

'Not really. He made a condition that if I were to marry Akriti, I had to receive a nod of agreement from my family as well; not just Neerav's father but also my father and mother. I took this as an opportunity to finally meet my parents after so many years. That's the reason I decided to keep Akriti under protection in my parents' house in Mumbai. So, we left Chandigarh for Mumbai, stopping in Delhi on the way to seek Neerav's father's blessings,' Rahul told her.

'I don't understand how Akriti's disappearance is related to Rahul's past. Does this imply that Rashid's team is behind this attack because their mission against our nation failed?' Neerav, who had sat quietly until now, finally spoke.

'But most of all, where could Akriti possibly be?' Rahul posed another question.

'Well, there could be numerous possibilities. One could be that Rashid's team kidnapped Akriti in revenge for Rashid's arrest. The other could be that Akriti is actually Afsana and on sensing danger, she decided to flee, but not before trying to seek revenge by bombing your car,' Rashi told him.

'Nothing you are saying convinces me. Okay, I was in love with her and didn't realize her intentions, but was the entire team so infatuated with her that no one—not a single person associated with the operation, not even Director Rajiv Jain—was able to sense it?' Rahul said.

Things were as muddled as they could be. 'Neerav, were you able to track Akriti's location through her cell phone?' Rahul turned to look at Neerav.

'The phone's location was changing continuously throughout the night, and in the morning the phone was discovered in a container lorry in Nashik. The phone might have been thrown into the vehicle to make us believe that Akriti was carrying it. It's not a normal thing to do. It could be the work of Rashid's gang,' Neerav suggested.

'Anyway, I have to get going,' Rashi told them, 'I'll meet you tomorrow with some more information.'

Before leaving, she said to Rahul, with mischief in her eyes, 'You are either a bad boyfriend or a bad officer.'

Even with all his available resources, Rahul felt powerless. It had been twenty-four hours since Akriti went missing. No one had any idea where she was. Was she really a spy or was there a Titanic conspiracy behind tagging her as an anti-Indian? Although there was enough evidence against her, Rahul refused to believe that she was guilty. He was determined to prove the theories incorrect.

~

It's been a day without you,
Then why does it seem like ages?
The memories are still loud,
You come in my pain,
You come in my gain,
My soul echoes your name at every sight,
Making me feel alone every night.
I draw your picture with crayons,
But there is no shoulder to lean on.
My heart aches to listen to you,
It cries helplessly to see you,
Distant landscapes fade into the sky
To say, 'I remember you.'
My life is a canvas without colours,

Like a TV without a remote to start it.
Where are you, my love, when will you come?
My tears demand an answer.

'I think you should go home. Your parents must be worried because you haven't informed them about the happenings since yesterday,' Neerav suggested.

'I was careless in my duties. I am so ashamed of myself,' Rahul said remorsefully.

'Rahul, don't worry. We'll get to the bottom of this matter, find the perpetrators and punish them. Please don't lose hope now. Even if others don't, I still believe in you, and I believe that you are a very capable intelligence officer. I have informed the director. He will definitely find a way to reach out to Akriti,' Neerav consoled him.

Neerav was hell-bent on knowing the truth that lay hidden in the pages of an unknown book.

Rahul reached home to be deluged with questions. His parents asked him where Akriti was and what had taken him so long. He avoided the grilling and went directly to his room. Karan went after him and talked to Rahul in his room.

'What happened? Is everything okay? Where is Akriti?'

'Karan, I am in no mood to answer questions right now. I'll explain everything when I feel up to it,' Rahul told him.

Rahul rested on the bed with his eyes closed, but despite his fatigue, he was unable to sleep. His parents were discussing him in the drawing room but he tried not to listen to them. Just when he fell asleep, Karan began knocking furiously on his door, 'Rahul, the CBI is here.' Rahul feared the worst and when he reached the drawing room, two uniformed men were waiting for him.

'Mr Rahul, we are here from the anti-corruption team, CBI. We have information that you have taken a bribe during an operation and let a spy, under the alias Akriti, escape. We have a warrant to search your house.'

Mr Rane looked confused, 'What is this all about, Rahul?'

'Will you please wait, Dad?' Rahul said. Then he spoke to the officer, 'There has been a mistake. Akriti has gone missing and the INA is searching for her. I am the head officer in this case. How could I possibly accept a bribe to help her flee?'

'I understand but the CBI suspects that you conspired with her. I request you to cooperate and let us carry out our search,' one of the officers told him.

They began searching every corner of the house, opening drawers and cupboards, scanning files and folders, but found nothing.

'I told you, Officer,' Rahul said sternly.

'Check the bathrooms too,' one officer commanded the other.

In no time, they recovered a stack of unaccounted cash from one of the toilet flush tanks. The stack was sealed in plastic and kept inside the tank so that no one would notice. Rahul was stunned beyond belief. He had no clue as to where the cash had come from or who had hidden it there.

'You are under arrest, Mr Rahul. Come along with us before we're forced to drag you.'

The smell of conspiracy was strong and evident after Rahul was incarcerated. A series of unfavourable events had rendered him weak, and loving Akriti was making him lose his mind. Love blinds you the moment it touches you—you can either live blissfully in its embrace or die besotted in its shadow. Except, you don't get to decide what happens to you.

~

Rahul was granted permission to make a phone call. He immediately dialled Neerav's number and explained what had happened. Neerav assured him that he would immediately inform the director and seek his help. A couple of hours later, Rahul was released on the request of the INA director, Rajiv Jain, who had spelled out that Rahul had been framed. However, the anti-corruption officer had given an ultimatum to Rahul which required him to prove himself innocent within a week.

On the way home, Rahul called Neerav to thank him. 'It's fine, Rahul. Also, I am very close to solving the case. I'll tell you in detail when I put the pieces together.' Neerav said, 'Now, you'd better hurry home for another round of interrogation.'

'I wish I had an option,' Rahul sighed.

~

'Here comes the culprit, this time without the officers. From the day you arrived, the stars of this house have been misaligned. Will you at least tell us what's happening?' Mr Rane shouted at Rahul before he could even enter the house.

'Dad, will you allow me to breathe, or should I go back? The officer didn't torture me as much as you are torturing me.'

'Is that how you talk to your parents? You have no manners even after all these years,' Mr Rane was furious.

This house hasn't changed a bit. I was and will always remain a soft target, Rahul gave up.

'Is Akriti a terrorist? What was the officer saying?' Rahul's mother interrupted them.

'I have no idea, Mom. She went missing the day we went out. Our team is trying to find out whether she was kidnapped or if she was involved in a conspiracy,' Rahul explained. He briefly described Operation Tusk to them, cautious not to reveal any confidential details.

'So, Akriti is a terrorist and you helped her escape?' his father questioned him.

'I haven't done anything. Someone tried to frame me. My friend, Neerav, is part of the team investigating who did it. The girl who came to see you, Karan,' Rahul said, looking at Karan, 'Rashi is an RAN agent and is trying to help us find out more about Akriti.'

'All I know is that owing to you, the CBI entered our house today. A terrorist wife, a scammer husband— maybe the child will be a politician,' his father said disapprovingly.

'You may say whatever you like,' Rahul ignored his father's baseless allegations.

'Have you informed Akriti's parents about what happened?' Rahul's mother asked.

'No. What could I have told them? That their daughter has been kidnapped because I left her alone in a car? Please forgive me for breaking the promise of protecting Akriti, no matter what,' Rahul said, angry at himself.

'What about this girl, Rashi? She did not tell us anything about working with the RAN,' her mother said. Then she asked Karan, 'Did Rashi tell you she's been meeting with Rahul frequently?'

'Mom, we haven't spoken in a while now. Why would she tell me who she's been meeting with? We are not seeing each other nor are we preparing to get married,' Karan said, irritated.

Rahul was so surprised at his mother's choice of questions that he said, 'Yes, Mother, I have been dating Rashi for a while now. I hope you don't have a problem, Karan?' Then he turned to look at Karan.

'Absolutely not. Go ahead with it. If you need any help, do let me know,' Karan smiled.

Rahul smiled back but deep within he was worried. Akriti had been missing for some days now, with no trace whatsoever. Was it the perfect crime or were Rahul and his team missing something? Anxiety lurked beneath the shadow of gloomy faces. *Every time I start missing you, I brood about not being together. I try to pacify myself by thinking that the worst is already over. But no matter what I do, loneliness casts its gloom, like a merciless, raging tornado. It sucks away my life's happiness and I feel the urge to embrace you. My heart is barely limping along, and there are moments when I feel delusional. There are times when I feel low and weak, lost, dazed and confused, almost as if I am nursing a permanent flu. This is the state of my life right now. Without you, things are not the same; for all the ups and downs, all this confusion, I know only I am to blame. However strong I may pretend to be on the outside, I am broken deep within. At first sight, nothing seems to be wrong but on introspection, my life now feels like a sad song.*

In the evening, Rahul and Karan were sitting in Rahul's room.

'Do you smoke?' Karan asked Rahul.

'I do. Do you have one?'

Karan nodded, 'Let's go for a walk if you like.'

Rahul and Karan were walking next to each other. Rahul felt himself relax in his elder brother's company. Karan and Rahul had never gotten along very well, owing to the constant comparisons they were subjected to as children. They did not hate each other as kids, but unfortunately, they didn't share any happy memories of their childhood together. While Rahul and Neerav had a very healthy relationship—fighting like a married couple, sharing like best friends, and having each other's backs like brothers—Karan and Rahul had nothing of the sort. So today, when Karan had suggested they go out for a smoke, Rahul was extremely pleased. Perhaps, the smoke of the cigarette would bring them closer together. 'Does Mom know that you smoke?' Rahul asked, as he lit a cigarette.

'Are you mad? She would've driven me out of the house if she knew,' Karan laughed.

'Does your girlfriend know that you smoke?' Karan asked as Rahul passed the cigarette to him.

'Yes, she knew me in and out,' Rahul's shoulders fell as he talked about her, 'I can't imagine what she must be going through.'

'Who are the people behind all this and what are they up to?' Karan asked worriedly.

'That's what Neerav is trying to find out. By tomorrow he should have the details. I just hope Akriti is safe.'

'Everything will be okay, Rahul,' Karan put one arm around his shoulder.

'Tell me something. Why did you choose to stay silent about my behaviour? I mean I robbed money because I wanted to buy a gift for Trisha, and I crashed the cycle on purpose,' Rahul had always wanted to know.

'Because your intentions were not as bad as their results turned out to be. We were kids. How could you have known that a motorcycle would run over my leg? How could you have known that Mom would need the money sooner than you'd imagined? You, anyway, would have replaced it after getting your pocket money,' Karan told him.

'Hmm, does Mom still keep money in envelopes?' Rahul asked, remembering that day.

'Why? Are you planning to steal some again?' Karan teased.

Taking a few notes from his wallet, Rahul said, 'No, I was hoping to return some, as an apology. Keep it in the envelopes where she keeps the money, will you?'

~

Is it a destination
or a quick walk on the sand?
Is there an indication
that the truth lies where I stand?
Is it really determination
when I can't even touch it with my own hand?
Is it a good intention
or part of some selfish plan?

Is it a mere observation
or the harsh reality?
Is it a passing situation
or a lasting bitter memory?
Is this a confession
or are my words losing their meaning?
Is it my imagination
that you will soon go away from me?

Rahul had impatiently waited for the sun to rise that morning. Last night, Neerav had informed him about some new information the INA had got access to. He'd asked Rahul to meet him so he could share the details. They'd decided to meet at a downtown cafe, so their whereabouts would be unknown.

Rahul had reached the cafe five minutes early and was impatiently waiting for Neerav to arrive. He had called Neerav again to ask him where he was.

'Yes, I am coming, bro. I'm not your sperm that would come so fucking fast. This sperm needs to cross Mumbai traffic during the rush hour. So be patient; I'll reach the cafe soon and reveal everything,' Neerav disconnected the call immediately.

Rahul's listlessness made him want to sink his nails into his skin and claw it off. It made him want to rip his hair from its roots. What was it that Neerav was about to reveal? Rahul felt the restlessness of a thousand whirlpools gushing in the pit of his stomach. *What had happened to Akriti? Who had kidnapped her? Why were they ruining her life and, most importantly, how was it all related to his past?*

When Neerav entered the cafe, Rahul stood up in anticipation, and then sat down. Neerav sat opposite him and placed a curious-looking file on the table. 'What's in the file?' Rahul asked, unable to hide his impatience.

'These are some confidential reports that Director Jain managed to get his hands on. They are related to Operation Tusk,' Neerav told Rahul.

'The file doesn't even look like it belongs to our department,' Rahul noticed.

'Exactly! The file belongs to RAN. In it is clearly mentioned that Rashi was the head of Operation Tusk. She was the one who was working along with her team to decode Rashid's background. But RAN couldn't get all the information related to him before us and as Director

Jain said, the team took it as an insult. Their pride was bruised.'

'So what if Rashi was the head?' Rahul still looked confused.

'Okay, let me put it this way. Rashid was sent to India as the lone spy from Pakistan. There is also no associate of Rashid known to be in India. All the information that he had managed to send to his country was either telephonic or through the business that we do with them. Also, the passport that Rashi showed us, which she claimed was Akriti's, was fake. In the midst of the chaos, it didn't occur to us to question why a spy would travel with their original passport. Spies are given fake passports when they are sent on a mission. The attack that happened at Akriti's house was not remotely related to Operation Tusk. It was a planned attack only on Akriti. Do you get it?' Neerav expounded.

'I can't believe it. Now I can fit the pieces together. First, Akriti goes missing from the highway and I meet Rashi there. She digs up my past by placing the note in the car herself after she has kidnapped Akriti. Then she must have thrown the phone into some vehicle so that we would not be able to trace Akriti.'

'Now you get it. She also has to be the one who planted the bomb in your car. But when you called her for help, she had to help you in order to appear innocent.'

'Mind-boggling. So we weren't searching for any real clues. She made us search for the ones she wanted us to find. But why would Rashi do all this?' Rahul was flabbergasted.

'I think it's a power struggle between the INA and RAN. That's all I can make of it,' Neerav said.

'I can't believe RAN would go to such an extent to win this war,' Rahul was shocked. 'Was she also the one behind planting the money in the flush tank?'

'I don't know about that,' Neerav said, 'but you can ask her yourself when she comes to meet us today.'

Rashi, let's unravel your history this time, Rahul thought.

~

If you had the chance, would you go back in time? Would you change your past? Stop yourself from doing something you shouldn't have? You may wish to erase the memories so that you don't have to remember the bad times; you may wish to tear off your own skin so that you would not remember the way my skin felt against yours. You may wish to burn the places you used to go so that you don't have to look at them again, but I won't let that happen; and when you're alone, I will hit you, and I will hit you hard. I'll crawl into your veins and eat you alive. I will crush your soul and leave you breathless. You will remember every single tear you've made others shed, and you'll feel a deep stab in your chest. You may dare to scream but no one will hear you; you are alone in this game and no one can help you—not even the one who holds your heart for you. You'll try to gasp for air but you'll not be able to utter a single word. The sound of your memories will break your heart; it'll leave you crushed at night when you fail to fall asleep. Remember, I had told you in the very first phase of this game that you cannot press the escape button to make a safe exit each time you find yourself struggling. You have to play this game, and I'll kill you in a thousand ways and make you feel nothing but pain. Remember, I am just seeking an opportunity to take revenge; for now I am the only devil and the only God. The extent of my rage has just begun and now I am going to be the enemy of your life. I, Rudra, the destroyer, am the ghost of your past, and I vow to haunt you until you die. Never forget what you did in the past and that it will come back to you in ways you cannot imagine.

Life is vindictive. It has a way of making you deal with what you make others go through.

Chapter 12

Day 1

'Where's Akriti?' Rahul asked as soon as Rashi was sitting in front of them.

'And how would I know that? Your girlfriend's on the run, remember?' Rashi said, mocking Rahul.

'Stop this game of pretence at once. I know everything—how you kidnapped Akriti while I was gone and carefully placed a note on her seat; how you planted a bomb in my glove compartment and then pretended to help me. That passport you showed us claiming to be Akriti's was fake too,' said Rahul, putting all the facts in front of her.

'Sad you figured it out so late, Intelligence Officer,' Rashi said scornfully.

'Why are you doing all this? I have never met you before and our jobs are strictly professional. You just can't take it personally. The fact that we accomplished Operation Tusk before RAN had nothing to do with you or your team. It wasn't a personal attack. But what you are doing to Akriti and me is a personal attack, and I can put charges against you for the same. It's not a war between RAN and INA, for God's sake.'

'I like your frustration,' Rashi smiled cunningly. 'Yes, it's not a war. It is pure revenge. What for? I am not in the mood to tell you. Now that the truth is out in the open, I challenge you: find your girlfriend or I will kill her. I give you four days, Mr Rahul, Assistant Central Intelligence Officer, to rescue your girlfriend—prove your worth—put your brains to work. Otherwise, you will lose Akriti forever.'

'What have you done with Akriti? Speak up, bitch,' Rahul could not control his fury.

'Mind your tongue, Intelligence Officer. Do you think I've so intricately designed my plan only to solve it for you at the end? Calling me a bitch proves how weak you are at this point. When a man doesn't have the patience to deal with shit, he calls women bitches. People like you, who call women bitches for overpowering men, are defeated cowards. Now stop wasting time. I have already declared an ultimatum of four days. Prove that you are a man and save your girl or pay the price for your deeds.'

Rashi was invincible.

'How did you manage to hide the money in Rahul's flush tank?' Neerav interrupted their conversation.

Looking at Rahul, Rashi answered, 'How could you forget that I was at your home to meet Karan along with my parents? Remember how you mentioned that it was unusual for the girl's family to visit the boy's family? That was it. I used your washroom, and I must say that hiding money inside a saree blouse hardly arouses suspicion. That was how I destroyed your integrity.'

'Is Akriti alive? Where is she?' Rahul pleaded with Rashi to tell him.

'Yes, very much. But for how long depends totally on you. When you stopped the car at the food mall and went inside, I kidnapped Akriti in the exact manner you just mentioned. I also gave the event an interesting climax—the bomb. I knew you would detect the bomb in the car and exit safely; you're at least that smart. However, you believed in my theories sooner than I expected. Now you're no more than a puppet in my game. You know it all but you can't prove it. You have heard it all but you can't make others listen.' Rashi told Rahul.

Rahul somehow wanted to hurt Rashi for everything she had done and tried to overpower her physically but Neerav stopped him. Frustration had taken a toll on him. 'There's no point in trying to harm me. I am the only person who knows where your girlfriend is. Prove your prowess, Officer. This is an ultimatum. You have four days to find your girlfriend alive or find her dead,' she said, showing him four fingers. After that, she left them more astonished than when she had come.

It never did end, did it? It was all still tumbling and rolling. Remember the hopscotch game that we played as kids where we made a hopscotch grid, numbering the squares from one to nine using chalk. You took a stone and tossed it in square one and then hopped over the square on a foot or both feet, following the hopscotch pattern all the way to square nine, but the game didn't end there. You had to turn around and come back, stop on square two, balance on one foot, and pick up the stone in square one and hop over. Didn't it teach you the rules of the game of life? We hop and reach our destination, and in the middle, we even hop over people, thinking they will be left behind. But that's not where the game ends. After reaching the last square, you have to come back, pick up the person while balancing your present, and pay the price for hopping over them. That's how the circle is completed. Rahul had started his return journey when he had decided to come back to Mumbai. Was it even his decision or the situation life had put him into, forcing him to turn around and pick up all the people he had hopped over, including his parents? But will he be able to complete the circle of life successfully, or, due to his past mistakes, will he be forced to give up his present?

~

I don't know what I have done. This girl seems to be out to destroy my happiness and integrity for no reason I can think of. Yet, she says she is seeking revenge—that she has a strong reason. What could that be? Why am I here? Oh God, please help me. Show me the way and forgive me for sins I have committed unknowingly. These thoughts plagued Rahul every second of his life.

If it was so easy to skip the levels and hurdles in life through cheat codes like a video game, God wouldn't have made us play his game called 'Life'.

Rahul reached home to find a package addressed to him lying on the table. He picked it up and went inside his room. Neerav had also come with him. Rahul tore the brown covering and found a letter inside. He opened it. What he read added another blow to his situation. Neerav, who saw Rahul's face turn pale, asked him what was written in it.

'It's a suspension letter,' Rahul declared.

'What?' Neerav was disturbed upon hearing this.

'Yes. Till the time the bribing charges are removed from my name and I am proven innocent, I am suspended.'

'Rashi is turning out to be a nightmare. The woman shoots bullets at regular intervals.'

'Why didn't Director Jain inform us about this? It's strange that the director kept such important information from us.'

Neerav called Director Jain immediately and had a word with him. The director's take on the matter was that he felt guilty about the suspension orders, as the ministry had had a meeting with the director first, after which the order was issued.

'I am sorry but I had little option. There was too much pressure on me, and I had no justification for what had happened, though we insiders know the bitter truth. Moreover, this wasn't the right time to reveal the truth to anyone as we have no proof. But let me talk to Rahul. Give him the phone if he's beside you.' Neerav handed the phone to Rahul.

'Yes, sir,' Rahul said.

'Rahul, I know it's not the right time to even ask how you are; I am sorry about what's happening. But I want you to work on this at a personal level and resolve it as soon as possible. Though I can't give you official orders to proceed, you have my support. We have no option other than finding Akriti and recording her statement to prove that you weren't at fault.'

'Yes, sir,' Rahul said before disconnecting the call.

'What happened? Is everything okay?' Karan asked, as he entered Rahul's room and saw their dejected faces.

Karan realized that he didn't know Rahul's friend, so he introduced himself.

'Hi, I am Karan, Rahul's brother.'

Neerav also introduced himself, 'Hi, I am Neerav. I am also Rahul's brother.'

Karan felt at sea and asked, 'So, has something bad happened?'

'Rahul has been suspended for taking bribes,' Neerav told him.

'Oh, no! What now?'

'Retirement, maybe?' Neerav tried to joke but Rahul waved him off.

'It'll get better, Rahul,' Karan tried to console him.

'I am at the abyss. It can only get better from here,' Rahul said, as he left the room.

~

Day 2

Rahul had asked Neerav to stay with him at his house rather than staying at the hotel. After having their morning tea, Rahul started a discussion on the thought that had kept him awake at night.

'She is not associated with Rashid. She seems to be a genuine RAN officer. Then how do we explain her abominable actions?' Rahul said to Neerav.

'Are her intentions connected with your past? That's what the note written by her was all about. Time and again, she has hinted towards it,' Neerav suggested.

'That's what I've been thinking too. If this is related to my past, it has to be connected to Trisha, my love in school. I can't think of any other person in my life with whom she would associate my past,' Rahul said.

'But what does Rashi have anything to do with Trisha? And why would she avenge Trisha after all these years?' Neerav was in doubt.

'Was I wrong in not informing Trisha before taking the drastic step of leaving everything behind? I just put the gift where we were supposed to meet and left without giving her any information,' Rahul spoke thoughtfully. At that time, he had felt that his action was justified. He had loved Trisha so much, it would have been difficult to leave her if he'd seen her before leaving. But now, he couldn't help looking back on that incident.

'From her perspective, you definitely did the wrong thing.'

The two of them thought for a while before Neerav spoke, 'If Rashi is the one plotting everything, I am sure she must have left a hint so that we can reach the place she wants us to. Why don't you talk to Karan? Maybe, he knows something about her that we don't?'

'You're right. I should have thought of this before. We should ask Karan about her,' Rahul agreed. Rahul called Karan and asked him whether he recalled anything that Rashi might have revealed regarding her own life.

'Nothing special as such,' Karan told them.

'Anything? Maybe where she lived or where she studied or anything about her friends?' Rahul asked.

'Yes, I think she told me that she studied at Holy Cross and stays near the school itself.'

The picture seemed clearer to Rahul now. Holy Cross. The school where Trisha had studied.

'I need to meet Rashi right away,' Rahul got up, determined to clear his doubts immediately. His battle was against time. Only two days remained.

~

'Is this related to Trisha? You are here to take revenge because I didn't inform her before leaving. This has nothing to do with RAN or INA. This is your personal war and you are here to avenge her. What I don't understand is, almost two decades later, why on earth would you want to dig up the past? And how on earth are you related to Trisha?' I am sure she has moved on. Then why do you want to fuck up the present?'

163

Rashi smiled at Rahul's perplexed expression but didn't say anything. Neerav said, 'You abducted Akriti because that was the only way you could hurt Rahul and avenge Trisha.'

Rahul added, 'I am cent per cent sure that the attack that happened at Akriti's house was planned by you and your colleagues. You were not targeting Akriti as an RAN officer to save her but as someone related to Trisha. You knew that hurting her would hurt me, and you did exactly that. You tried to frame her, tried to make her look bad in my eyes. You deluded me into believing she tried to kill me. And you did this for revenge. Your only motive is to torture me and ruin my peace.'

'Now that we know your intentions, you'd better tell us where Akriti is. You gave us four days and we are here on the second day itself, exposing you.'

'You've got it wrong, officers. The ultimatum is not about you finding out about my intentions. It is about you finding Akriti for yourselves. Even if this is about Trisha, does that help you in finding Akriti?' Rashi raised her eyebrows and answered. Calm and composed, she was sure of her every step. Not only hers, she was confident about Rahul's moves too. He was, after all, a pawn in her game, and she was playing him as she desired.

'May I . . . if you have both finished?' Neerav questioned.

When both Rashi and Rahul allowed Neerav to speak, he asked Rashi, 'Give me a little clarity on this subject. How are you associated with Trisha? Who are you? And after so many years, what are you going to get by proving that Rahul was wrong in abandoning Trisha? Do you realize how stupid your motive sounds—punishing a man for a small mistake he committed as a kid? You are ruining a person's life, so he should at least know how you are connected with his past—how you are connected with Trisha. Throw some light on that, will you?'

Realizing that she was the master of the game in which the two officers sitting in front of her were helpless pawns, Rashi decided to reveal her deck of cards. 'Yes, each one of my assaults is for Trisha. I want Rahul to be defeated and broken. I want him to know that leaving Trisha alone on a park bench waiting for him was the biggest mistake of his life, and that he will pay for it with every bit of his life. Because I am Trisha, the girl who loved Rahul with all her heart. I am the Trisha of your past, the girl who received betrayal for loving a boy so immensely.'

'This can't be true,' Rahul was stunned to hear what the girl sitting in front of him had just said.

'Don't waste your time, Rahul. There are more surprises waiting at your doorstep. And remember, the clock behind you will not stop ticking. Tick. Tick. Tick,' Rashi said, and Rahul thought he saw a tear in her eye.

Strike a note; you have to play this game and I'll kill you in a thousand ways, and make you feel nothing but pain. Remember, I am just seeking an opportunity to take revenge, for remember I am the only devil and the only God. I am your past. And when the past seeks revenge, it can destroy anything that comes in its way—it can defeat your present— it can jeopardize your future. That is the wrath of the past— it is invincible.

~

After they had reached home, Rahul and Neerav were once again sitting on Rahul's bed, processing the news they'd just been given. Rahul was holding his head in his hands, unable to trust the veracity of Rashi's words. Every confrontation with that woman was so excruciating.

'Do you really think she is Trisha or is she bluffing?' Neerav asked.

'No, she can't be Trisha. Rashi looks nothing like Trisha,' Rahul told him.

'Don't compare on the basis of the facial features she had fifteen years ago. You should check the photo on my driving licence, taken around twelve or thirteen years ago. Even I don't recognize myself in that picture.'

Neerav showed him his driving licence and Rahul couldn't help smiling.

'You resemble Kasab.'

'That's why, bro, do not go on looks. Consider this thoroughly.'

'This isn't just about the facial features. Trisha wouldn't grow up to be someone like Rashi. Trisha was my first love. I cannot believe the tender girl I knew could turn out like this. The sense of understanding and maturity she had at that age would never transform her into a woman like Rashi. There are no similarities between the two girls at all,' Rahul explained.

'Should we ask her a few questions that only the two of you knew? For instance, any embarrassing episode like the one you shared with Akriti when you were caught naked by Akriti's mom.'

Only Neerav could find humour in the gravest of situations. Rahul was not very pleased about it, 'We were covered with a blanket.'

'Of course you were,' Neerav laughed, 'but do you have similar memories with Trisha?'

'Not exactly but somewhat.'

'What the fuck? Are you serious? Have you been a pervert since the beginning?'

'I'll kick your arse. Trisha and I weren't sleeping together. It was a harmless kiss in the park. Karan had seen us do it,' Rahul disclosed.

'Oh man! I haven't even hugged a girl at thirty and you had your first kiss in school. Now I get it, all right.

It's your karma, Rahul. Now your karma is kissing you back,' Neerav grinned.

'Are you done? Shall we get back to business?' Rahul said irritably. 'Listen carefully, Neerav, since this is a personal attack, I want you to ask the director to stop the official investigation. The spy from Pakistan has been arrested. There is no need to proceed officially,' Rahul continued.

Neerav was about to call Director Jain when he received a WhatsApp text from the director himself.

Check the news as soon as possible. I have sent you the link and forwarded it to Rahul as well.

'Rahul, check your WhatsApp. The director has sent a link,' Neerav said, and opened the link. Rahul also opened the link on his phone.

Assistant intelligence officer Rahul booked for bribery charges in a secret operation; alleged to have set Pakistani spy free. The investigation bureau found the money in his flush tank when they raided his house. No signs of arrest yet.

Yet another appalling surprise from Rashi was exposed, and from the look on Rahul's face, it was evident he didn't like it.

The man who had lived his professional life with pride and integrity, who was one of the most eminent officers of the INA, was not only suspended but also publicly accused of treason. Rahul was devastated on reading the article that mentioned all the allegations against him and called him a quisling. Throughout his career, Rahul had sacrificed every bit of himself for his country. He had done his duty with diligence and honesty, and now, in return, he received suspension and public shame. This was no longer a game. His reputation was at stake; his integrity had been called into question, while love continued to play vile tricks with him.

Chapter 13

Day 3

You don't need a degree in psychology to see that someone is lying, and there was no doubt in Rahul's mind that Rashi was making everything up. The fact that she had abducted Akriti was believable. However, her claims to be Trisha sounded groundless to him. But he had no proof and had to give in to the situation. Rahul felt anguish over the media's harassment and persecution, but he preferred to stay away from all of it. Rashi had managed to make a noise that had begun to crescendo.

Rahul had even considered seeking help from his parents as they knew Rashi's family, but he decided against it. They were very displeased with him and would never agree to help. The next morning, Rahul's dad berated him, 'You'd better find that girl—Akriti—and leave immediately. Tell her parents that you have our permission to get settled together. But just spare us the trouble of living with us and making it any more of a nightmare than it already is.'

Rahul had nothing to say in return. He did not wish to defend himself any more, so he went back to his room where Neerav had already overheard their conversation.

'We need to find out where Rashi stays,' Rahul told Neerav.

'We have no option but to request Karan to extract that information from your parents,' Neerav said.

They were doubtful whether Karan would agree to extort information from his parents. After all, Karan had always been the obedient son who was known to never break the rules. When they confronted him, he agreed without a moment's hesitation. The whole day he kept trying to figure out ways to approach his father, and after a lot of effort, he was able to obtain Rashi's address. He handed over the information to Rahul.

Day 4

'Rahul, are you sure we're doing the right thing? Barging into a girl's house without permission? I mean, what if the door is locked? Can you knock the door down like Daya in *CID*?' Neerav was dubious. Rahul and Neerav had both navigated to the desired location once they had the much-needed information.

'I am not backing off now. If we want to find out anything about Rashi, this is the only place that can give us answers. You can either come with me or go back home. The choice is yours.'

'Of course, you are my Suppandi and I am your Maddy. I will do as you say, like a good friend,' Neerav snickered.

As the two of them drove closer to their destination, Rahul's biggest nightmare was coming true. He was almost at the same location where Trisha had stayed, and the map took them to the exact lane where her apartment had been. The voice on Google Maps declared that they had reached their destination, and it was the same building where Rahul remembered Trisha living. Karan had given them no information about the flat number. Although Rahul could not recall Trisha's flat number, he knew the floor, and when they reached the wing, he saw a familiar nameplate on one of the flats.

'Oh God! Now I remember Dad mentioning Rashi's surname. The Pathak family was supposed to come home.'

'So?' Neerav looked confused.

'Trisha's surname was also Pathak,' saying this, Rahul tried the door to the flat but it was locked.

'Let's take a modest route by asking the watchman,' Neerav suggested, and walked towards the watchman who sat reading a newspaper in his cabin.

'Bhaiya, can you tell us whether the Pathak family still stays here?' Neerav questioned.

'Yes. But no one is there at their house right now. You are?' the watchman asked.

'We are Trisha's friends. No problem, thank you,' Neerav replied.

~

Rashi's story was like a maze for Rahul. He had tried many ways but all the gates had been bolted. Yet, he was compelled to solve the maze because one of the paths led to the love of his life.

'I know what to do. There's only one solution. All this time we've followed her footsteps; now she will have to follow ours,' Rahul told Neerav.

'What are you up to?'

'I'll call her to the same place where Trisha and I used to meet; the same spot by the lake in the garden. She claims to be Trisha, doesn't she? Let's see how she gets there. Our meeting spot was privy to only Trisha and me,' Rahul smiled.

'And Karan who saw you kissing,' Neerav winked.

Rahul had dialled Rashi's number and asked her to come to the place where he and Trisha used to meet. He had not given away more details. All the masked probabilities would be exposed, leaving behind the traces of truth and nothing else. Slowly but steadily, the pieces of his past were fitting together to form a complete picture, which would put an end to all the complexities he had gone through in the past few days. With only a few hours left before the fourth day ended, he was still in the game and he would prove that it was not over yet.

'Are you sure she won't come?' Neerav asked once they reached the garden and walked towards the same spot where Rahul had left his past incomplete. He had never thought that life would bring him back to the same square. But here he was, with memories flashing in his head. He remembered how innocent loving someone at such a young age had felt. He remembered how he'd once loved a girl with an angel face. He pictured Trisha waiting for him to surprise her with a gift. He pictured her getting up to leave, with the dejected face of a jilted lover. Neerav sensed that Rahul was lost in his thoughts. His eyes had become moist.

'Are you okay?' Neerav asked.

'Yes, it's just that this place reminds me of her,' Rahul told him.

'Do you still love her?'

'No, but I once did, with all my heart. Now we've grown up and left those years behind us. I hope Trisha is happy wherever she is. I just want to know what Rashi is up to,' Rahul said pensively.

Before Neerav could think of a suitable response, they saw Rashi walking towards them. With every step she took towards them, Rahul grew more perplexed. When he thought he had reached the pinnacle of the mountain, he slipped hard and fell back to the ground. He was now mentally and emotionally incapacitated. 'You didn't expect me here, did you?' Rashi said with her signature smile.

Rahul was too distraught to speak. How did this woman know everything?

'Why don't we sit here again? Let's kiss each other the way we did before, forgetting the world around us. Why did you leave me waiting, Rahul? The sadness of that waiting has killed me for years. Remember, this was the place where you had left your gift for me?'

Rahul interrupted her as if some thought had just struck him. He smiled and broke his silence, 'Before kissing, let's go to the stall where we used to eat pani puri for a snack. What do you say?'

Rashi looked puzzled and Rahul knew that she had no information on the subject. 'Why don't you lead?' Rahul said, gesturing to Rashi to show them the direction.

But Rashi only walked till the exit and stopped, not knowing which direction to head towards.

Rahul smiled and asked her to guide them, but she didn't move a step. 'You were lying. You're not Trisha. I loved her and even though we parted ways, I know that she wasn't a girl who could go to such extremes to hurt someone. Sadly, before you came here, your watchman gave us all the information we needed,' Rahul finally told Rashi.

~

When both Neerav and Rahul had walked towards the watchman's cabin and asked whether the Pathak family stayed in the same apartment, the watchman had nodded affirmatively, and when he asked them who they were, Rahul had conned him by saying they were Trisha's friends.

'Trisha madam? But she doesn't stay here.'

Rahul was sharp to catch on to the watchman's reply. If Rashi claimed to be Trisha, the watchman wouldn't have said that she didn't stay there. It was clear that Rashi was tricking them.

'Oh! We were such great friends in school. Can you tell us where she stays?' Rahul asked, eager to find out the truth.

'I don't know where she stays,' the watchman finally replied.

Rahul thought he had almost got there but the watchman had no clue about Trisha's whereabouts.

'So who stays here, then?' Neerav asked.

'Her sister, Rashi.'

An after-storm silence filled the air that surrounded them. Rashi was like a storm that had passed, destroying everything but Rahul's will. Rahul had sought answers and, having obtained them, he had called Rashi to the same place where he used to meet Trisha, thinking she wouldn't know where to come; but even after she did, Rahul had peeled away the layers of falsehood and deceit Rashi had used to cover her true being.

~

'So, is there anything you'd like to say, Ms Rashi? How does it feel to be exposed?' Rahul asked scornfully.

'Yes, I am Rashi, Trisha's sister. But Rahul, finding that out doesn't make you a prodigy. You think you are here because you cracked it. No, you are here because I wanted you to be here. I wanted you to be at the place where you left my sister heartbroken. I wanted you to recall the injustice you did to a fourteen-year-old heart madly in love.' She continued, 'The day we failed in the operation to imprison Rashid, and your team cracked it, was the day I heard your name again, after so many years. I instantly knew you were the same guy who broke my sister, Trisha, emotionally. That was when I decided to knock your brains out, to torture you, to humiliate you, to strip your integrity and to leave you anguished, with the help of my friends who were in my team. And that's what I did.'

'You planted a bomb in his car. That isn't torture. It's attempted murder,' Neerav said angrily.

Rashi laughed, 'If an intelligence officer cannot detect a bomb, he might as well die.'

'Where is Trisha?' Rahul's voice was full of guilt.

'Sorry, did I hear Trisha instead of Akriti?' Rashi asked with a tone of sarcasm in her voice.

'It's not funny, Rashi. Where is she?'

'After fifteen years, do you finally realize that it was not funny? Leaving a girl like that. You are the epitome of selfishness,' Rashi said angrily.

'Rashi, will you please tell me where Trisha is, and is she okay?' Rahul pleaded with her.

'Why should I tell you that?' Rashi was still not moved.

'Because I am requesting you,' Rahul's tone softened, his eyes looked worried. He needed to know if she was okay.

'Trisha is in an asylum,' Rashi finally told him.

~

Eighteen years before

Trisha was a strong cup of coffee in a world that was drunk on beer. Relationships are hard to handle, they say, but for her, they were as simple as ABC. Not only did she share good relationships with friends but also with her family.

Trisha and Rashi were the best of sisters. They were each other's heartbeats. Rashi was older than Trisha, and Trisha always looked up to her for advice. Rashi protected her sister and wanted the best for her. They were so close that sometimes, their mother worried about how they would live in separate houses after marriage, to which the girls would happily say, 'We'll ask the boys to come stay at our place. We don't want to marry if there are so many restrictions on girls after marriage. Nobody can separate us. They won't dare! Why do only girls need to adjust after marriage? Tell boys to leave their parents and stay with us. Why should we leave our parents if they can't leave theirs? Who made such stupid traditions? We'll change all these when we grow up. We'll make our husbands leave their parents and stay with our family. It has to be the new rule. If they want us to leave our family, then they also have to leave theirs. Tit for tat. And if they don't agree, then we will take so much dowry from them that we can insure you with that money. We'll change all the traditions when we grow big.'

'You are both too small to think about all this. You don't know how the world is,' was their mother's signature reply, whenever they tried to square accounts.

Their camaraderie sometimes worried their parents, because when someone would hurt Trisha in school, Rashi paid them back in full, and when someone would tease or upset Rashi, Trisha knew how to get even with them. However, looking at their love for each other, they felt proud of the way they had raised their children.

Everything was smooth sailing until Trisha's life was turned upside down.

~

Earlier that day, Sandy had handed a letter to Trisha. After reaching home, Trisha had locked her room and taken the letter from her bag and smiled to herself. Since the day that Karan had seen them kissing, she had pretended to be angry so that Rahul would confess his love for her. After reading the letter, she had tears in her eyes. She had immediately gotten in touch with Rahul, and they had decided to meet on Monday. But on Monday, when she reached the garden, Rahul was nowhere to be seen, although she spotted a gift-wrapped box at the place they used to sit. She looked around for him but to no avail. Then she went to the pani puri stall where they generally ate and asked the vendor if he'd seen Rahul.

'Yes, he came here but he left shortly after. He'd eaten a lot of pani puris,' the man behind the stall had told her.

'Did he say anything?'

'Just that he was going somewhere far away and would take time to return. I even asked if it was some special trip but he didn't answer.'

Trisha felt betrayed because Rahul had claimed to love her, and now he was nowhere to be seen. It was likely that he'd left for some place without bothering to tell her where. She had no inkling about where the love of her life had gone.

Trisha went to a PCO booth nearby, and plucking up courage, she dialled Rahul's landline. She gave three missed calls, which was their code, in the hope that Rahul would pick up the call if he was home. But when she called a fourth time, Rahul's mother picked up and Trisha disconnected the call immediately. She tried a couple more times but had no luck. Even after returning home, she tried dialling Rahul again, but this time, Mr Rane picked up. Rahul's unexplained absence distressed Trisha. She kept the little panda stuffed toy that Rahul had gifted her on the study table as an air of melancholy surrounded her.

You told me I was the girl of your dreams, but you stopped dreaming. I don't want to believe that there's a world where you can exist without me, she thought, as she went to sleep with lost hopes. Tender feelings and bad timing make for the most painful combination.

To be left without a goodbye or an explanation is the worst thing that can happen to a lover. Rashi watched as her younger sister's smile slowly faded away. If things were not already bad enough, Trisha was blamed for Rahul's disappearance. She was told that it was because of her that he had left home forever. It was only then that Trisha discovered that Rahul had stolen money to buy her a gift. The humiliation continued for more than a month and she began to hate herself. Girls called her a slut because they had somehow heard about Rahul and Trisha kissing in the park. They commented on how she was so demanding as a girlfriend that Rahul had had to steal money to buy her a gift. Trisha found herself becoming the topic of whispered conversations in hallways, and it was at these times that she wished she were dead. Trisha was disconsolate because, on the one hand, she missed her boyfriend who'd not cared to tell her before leaving, and, on the other hand, she was held guilty for crimes she'd never committed. Somebody was efficiently spreading rumours about her wherever she went. This was making her life impossible.

You can't put too much pressure on a fourteen-year-old. Trisha forced herself to smile every day. She tried to be happy despite the cruel environment around her. Then, when it became too much of a task, all of a sudden, she stopped smiling.

Rahul had hurt her like no one else had. That was the time when Rashi realized she had lost someone close to her—a friend, and a family member. Sadness swept over Rashi the day her sister lost her purpose in life. Rashi forced herself to smile, but no optimism took over from the grief she went through as she watched her sister suffer at such a tender age, when she didn't even understand what life is about. When Rahul planted flowers inside her, Trisha had thought he would water them too. Silly her—they died.

Chapter 14

Present day

Rahul was grief-stricken upon hearing about Trisha. He could not fathom how his leaving her could have impacted her life so deeply. 'Who spread these rumours about her being responsible for me running away?' Rahul wanted to know.

'It was a boy from your school. He not only tortured her whenever they passed each other, he made sure that every person viewed her as a slut. He publicized the kiss in and around our school, our locality and her tuitions, through his friends. Trisha found it difficult to go to school or attend tuitions, and eventually, she stopped going. We changed her school, but you know, when a girl is good-looking, there are boys who try to dig up information related to her, and her character was crushed each and every time. It was then that we noticed Trisha was not just unhappy; she was suffering from depression. When she was blamed for the money you robbed, and demeaned for being a terrible girl, she was unable to take it. And that too for a few thousand rupees.'

Rashi continued, 'I don't care what situation you were in, but because of you, my family's situation disintegrated. You should have been more responsible.'

'Who was that person, Rashi? Why are you hiding his identity? I want to know right away,' Rahul was furious.

But Rashi ignored him. 'She started behaving differently. She found it difficult to make friends. On many occasions, she tried to harm herself. I can still recall the day I saw her dancing on her bed, and I thought that she'd finally found something to make her happy, but then as soon as she noticed me, she started throwing things around. Doctors told us that her behaviour was not normal any more. She'd had a nervous breakdown. We were advised to take her to an asylum. I lost my smile because my sister was my happiness. I felt weak because Trisha was my strength. The feats I achieved professionally could not fill the void of my sister's absence—nothing could make up for the loss of my best friend. Sometimes, you should choose your actions very carefully because you never know what damage they can do to a person. Your act of leaving made an indelible mark on her life. She felt that if she ever loved someone, they would leave her some day. She always smiled when she slept as if she were lost in the perfect dream, but when she woke up, she could not bring herself to face the harsh realities of the cruel world in front of her. What you did to her altered her life completely,' Rashi said with tears in her eyes.

'Please tell me the name of that person, Rashi. Why won't you tell me?' Rahul begged.

'Do you really want to know?' Rashi looked at him. Rahul nodded.

'It was your elder brother, Karan,' Rashi finally told him.

Rahul was devastated on hearing that. He could never imagine Karan doing such a thing in his wildest dreams. He only saw the beauty of the long-bodied fish and admired its teeth and dark eyes and how its fin cut through the water like a hot knife through butter; it was only when he let it get close enough to bite, that he realized the fish was a shark.

'The good thing is that Trisha will be released from the asylum in a week's time.' Rashi turned towards Rahul, 'Anyway, you've already wasted time hearing the background story. You should concentrate on saving your girlfriend. There isn't much time left.'

'Are you serious?' Rahul was astounded by her indifference.

'Yes, very much so. The torture, the pain and the humiliation . . . you have to go through it all. You have to strive for what you want, just like my sister had to. She never got what she deserved. Whether you get what you deserve depends on you.'

Rahul shook his head, 'That is not justified. What is the difference between you and Karan? Whatever he did years ago, you are doing exactly the same. You are also doing atrocious things to seek revenge for a dear one. Your methods are profoundly wrong. How can you become the thing you once hated? I agree that Trisha shouldn't have been treated the way she was, but I had no clue that this was happening here in her world. I wish that I had never run away; that I'd been there for Trisha, but the past cannot be rewritten. I want to apologize for all that she and her family had to go through. But Rashi, I had run away for my own reasons. I have already told you my story.' He continued, 'I am sorry for Trisha. I really am. There is nothing I would not do to go back in the past, if only to comfort her. I want to also apologize on Karan's behalf. But you must understand that you cannot inflict atrocities on someone else to avenge your sister. When a person goes through a certain trauma, he makes sure that he doesn't pass on that trauma to someone else, as he knows how it feels to be there. But you are getting carried away. Revenge is not a solution, and it has never worked. Anyhow, you have already crushed me in all the ways you could. Now by doing all this, if you want to prove that I am weak, do so, but that doesn't prove that you are strong. I would never want someone to go through what Trisha went through. Trisha will be released from the asylum in a very short time. She'll need you by her side; she'll need your love and support. From knowing Trisha when we were together, I can confidently say that had you been in her place, she would never have taken such drastic steps to seek revenge. Instead, she would have cared for you. Don't you think so?'

To heal a wound, you need to stop touching it. Rashi realized that Rahul's ignorance of the matter and his apologies were all genuine. Trisha would not be proud if she knew what Rashi had done in order to avenge her condition. Rashi decided, at last, to forgive him.

'Dude, you have become that guy from the *Neelam* show in the movie *Kuch Kuch Hota Hai* who ditched Suparna. Without informing, you just left. No one asked what happened to Suparna,' Neerav said, laughing on the way back home when Rahul was steaming with anger.

'How can you stay so fucking calm in every bloody situation?' Rahul revved the car as he raised his voice.

'You should also use coconut oil; it'll be good for you,' Neerav continued in his irrepressible style.

'As of now, Karan needs it to apply on his whole body. I am not going to spare him,' Rahul declared.

~

Rahul had asked Karan to wait near the highway close to their house saying that he needed him for some urgent work. When Rahul and Neerav reached the highway, they saw Karan standing talking to someone on the phone. Rahul fumed as he parked the car; Neerav knew that terrible things would follow. Before Karan had time to process the situation, Rahul knocked him down with one blow. Karan managed to straighten up. One swift punch on Karan's jaw whipped his head backwards and he fell again. Karan tried to ask why Rahul was hitting him, but Rahul continued hitting him until he was satisfied. Karan tried to defend himself but did not fight back.

When Rahul was done, he finally told Karan the cause of his fury. 'How could you have behaved like a moron, Karan?' Rahul was furious.

'I am so sorry, Rahul. I was trying to get back at her. Sandy had told me how you had wanted to buy a present for her so I'd assumed she was demanding. However, I only discussed the kiss with my friends. I didn't know that would lead to so many rumours that would taint Trisha's image. Sandy also told me that he'd suggested you run away, but never thought you would actually do it. So when I got to know this, it troubled me and whenever I saw Trisha, I tried to get even with her. You have to understand I was a kid too, Rahul. I did not know how adversely this would affect Trisha. There was nothing serious to it. My insults were innocuous, and as a teenager, I couldn't understand that it would spoil her life. Oh God! I am so sorry,' Karan was remorseful.

'You think it wasn't serious! You are a ruthless human being, Karan. No one stopped you as a child, and everything you did was considered right; whereas whatever I did was labelled wrong, even if we did the exact same thing! Every little thing that you escaped as a child gave you the courage to take such cruel steps. You knew that whatever the outcomes of your actions were, Mom and Dad would still support you. Despite that, I thought you were good at heart because you had kept my secrets. How immature could you have been! Shouldn't you have thought once before making a girl's life miserable? She's in a fucking asylum, Karan!' Rahul screamed.

'Rahul, I am so sorry. Is there any way I could apologize to her? I had absolutely no idea of what she was going through,' Karan said, wiping away the sweat from his forehead. Karan was upset. His immaturity had landed a fourteen-year-old in an asylum. It would take years for Karan to be able to forgive himself.

The argument continued between the brothers until Karan broke down in front of Rahul. Rahul realized that he should not delay in rescuing Akriti. Rashi had revealed the location where she had kept Akriti for the past few days. Rahul needed to get there as fast as he could. Karan and Neerav accompanied him.

～

For a moment, Rahul thought that Rashi had given in because she wanted Rahul and Trisha to be together, but later he realized that all she had wanted for him was to understand the consequence of an irrational action and a hasty decision. That was the reason she hadn't hurt him physically in the process of seeking revenge. But by clearing the dust of the past, you can't allow it to settle on your present. So although he felt terrible for Trisha, and prayed she would be okay, he knew that Akriti was his present and that he had to rescue her as soon as possible.

The indicator on the speedometer kept fluctuating, and the second hand on the clock kept revolving faster. Rahul had only a couple of hours left before he would see her. His heart was racing faster than both the speedometer and the hands of the clock. He could not decide whether he should have thanked Rashi for finally revealing the details of the location where she had kept

Akriti or berated her for keeping her there for five days without food and water. So, he hadn't said anything and left soon after the details had been provided by Rashi. As of now, he pressed his foot on the accelerator, eager to find Akriti as soon as possible. *The past few days have been difficult, especially since you've not been here with me, but no matter how far away you are, our love will find a way. I eagerly anticipate the day when we will get back together, as I miss your tender touch, your kiss, and most of all your hands as you caress my body. We were created for each other to ease each other's pain and sorrow, and to replace our sadness with love and happiness. I will love you eternally and unconditionally. I miss you more than words can convey, and my love will travel any distance to be close to you. I will find you soon, Akriti.*

Rahul entered Igatpuri, and navigating with the help of Google Maps, he reached the location of the building that Rashi had informed him about. Rahul had never been there and it terrified him—the idea that someone could live in this very building. It was deserted with ruins surrounding it—an edifice that emitted a frightening silence. Beside the front door, he noticed an empty space where a window once stood, now containing threatening remnants of sharp glass. He unlocked the door. Rahul reached the tenth floor where Akriti was incarcerated. There was a big fat lock on the entrance to the hall. He opened it with the set of keys that Rashi had given him.

From there, looking down, the whole structure appeared monstrous. Four interminable walls and a staircase leading to the foggy sky: like a house straight out of a horror movie. Nobody could have escaped a prison like that. He tried many rooms on the tenth floor, but he only encountered dust, cobwebs and graffiti on the walls. He shouted Akriti's name several times, but the rooms remained silent.

Had Rashi misdirected him? Had she not forgiven him yet? Terrible thoughts were racing through his head when he tried the last room on the floor, breaking down the door. And there she was, lying in a corner of the room, lifeless.

'Akriti . . . get up . . . get up . . .' Rahul kept repeating the words hoping she would hear. She opened her eyes for a few seconds and attempted to get up, but she couldn't. To her, the world was a blur of colours mixing with other colours and objects fusing together in front of her eyes. She lifted her hand to her head, wincing slightly. Her body felt weak, her eyelids felt heavy and then there was nothing, except the silence of the darkness.

~

'Doctor, is she fine? What's wrong with her?'

Rahul and Neerav had immediately taken her to the nearest hospital.

'What happened to her? It seems as though she hasn't eaten anything in the last four to five days. Also, her body is dehydrated because of no liquid intake. She has marks of a struggle from trying to free herself. There are other marks on her hands and legs almost as if they were tied with ropes. This might be a police case.'

'We are from the INA. We'll take care of it,' Rahul showed his identification card.

The day that Rashi had followed Rahul's car, she had abducted Akriti by knocking her out before Rahul could return from the food mall. Rashi had made her lie down on the back seat of her car so that she couldn't be seen from a distance. When Rahul had left for Mumbai, she had taken her to the isolated building in Igatpuri, tied her up and locked her in the room without food or water. Akriti had tried to free herself, which was evident from her scars, but after a point, she no longer had the strength to escape.

Rahul was extremely concerned because Akriti's condition was critical.

'We are injecting glucose into her body through a saline drip. She should gain consciousness in a few hours; however, we need to keep her under observation for another forty-eight hours.' the doctor assured Rahul.

Rahul was overwhelmed and couldn't thank the doctor enough. He had thought that he had lost Akriti, and this assurance certainly gave him strength. Every second and every minute in the last five days, weird thoughts had haunted his mind, and that strange feeling of losing someone close had made him weak. However, after overcoming all the struggles, there they were: so close, yet so far. Rahul's happiness resided in Akriti's soul, and he desperately wanted to look into her eyes again and say how much he loved her and cared for her. He desperately wanted to hold her hands and give her everything she deserved; he wanted to apologize for whatever suffering she had gone through because of his past. He had realized that it is impossible to put your past behind you and forget about it, because its shadow lurked in your present. Your past was always there, building and rebuilding your character, your soul and your life. Karan, who got the necessary medicines prescribed by the doctor, went inside the room and placed them beside Akriti. He looked at her and felt sorry. He knew he was to blame for her critical condition. Karan went outside and sat beside Rahul, holding him by his shoulder and giving him strength. That moved Rahul to tears, and he hugged him back tightly.

'I am really sorry, Rahul. Please forgive me. I know that I've done horrid things, but if you forgive me, then I can consider forgiving myself. I may not have been good at showing my affection, but I have always loved and cared for you, even when we were kids,' Karan said through his tears. Rahul hugged Karan because he needed his elder brother more than anything right now.

'You look like two brothers directly out of a Bollywood film who've met after long years of separation.' Neerav never missed an opportunity to mock Rahul, and both Karan and Rahul laughed.

After almost four hours, when Akriti finally opened her eyes, Rahul's happiness knew no bounds. He ran into her room and stood in front of her. She was resting half-seated with the support of a pillow. He immediately hugged her and the two started sobbing in each other's arms.

'I was afraid you'd leave,' Rahul said crying.

Akriti shook her head, 'How could I? You'd promised to hold my clammy hands forever, remember?' Rahul nodded and the two of them embraced again while Karan and Neerav beamed happily outside the door.

Don't you dare give up on this life. Not now, not tomorrow, not ever, Rahul said with his eyes without saying a word.

Not while you keep loving me like this, Akriti's eyes said in reply.

'First the brothers uniting, now the lovers uniting— we are all recreating Bollywood films,' Neerav joked again.

Rahul stood up from the bed and unexpectedly got down on his knees and kissed Akriti's hand, despite the insulin drip. He could have proposed to her a hundred times but he'd never thought that he would do it in a hospital room.

'You had told me to do it in a unique way. What could be more unique than a hospital?' Rahul laughed, 'Balloons, roses, hearts, candlelit dinners and gifts are too mainstream, don't you think? Like a devoted fan who refuses to wash the hand touched by his hero, I refuse to give up on you once you enter my life. I love you.'

'I love you too, Rahul. I promise you that you could take all the drugs in the world, kiss all the sexy girls you meet, drink hard liquor all night long and dance with the nymphs of another world, but you would never find the same high you found in me. I love you so much, baby,' Akriti laughed and Rahul joined her. They embraced each other.

'Akriti, don't believe him. Remember, he said this to the last girl too, they broke up and he is still alive and telling the same lies to you.' Neerav was trying his best to spoil their moment. That's what friends are for! If they don't spoil your moments, you need to cross-check if they are your real friends.

'Why are you even my friend?' Rahul said in frustration.

'Hey! Don't forget, Suppandi, that I am your Maddy. I may tease you and irritate you, but I am also your most loyal friend,' Neerav claimed proudly.

Karan came closer to Rahul and Akriti and held their hands in his, saying, 'I think it's time to go home. A new life awaits you, bhabi.'

Rahul looked at Karan and smiled at his sensitive gesture.

'No . . . no . . . it cannot end without a kiss. Come on, Officer. Kiss her right away,' Neerav added.

'Are you serious? Here, in the hospital?' Rahul was sceptical, but Neerav was adamant and insisted that they kiss.

Akriti held her breath, and Rahul held her hands in his. The moment sent a sweet shudder down her spine and she lifted her face to look at him. Rahul's eyes met her gaze and he lowered his face to hers. For a fraction of a second, his mouth brushed her lower lip, like the touch of butterfly wings.

'. . . and they kissed to live happily ever after. Once again in front of Karan,' Neerav announced, as they parted their lips.

It wasn't the end because together, people can even make forever seem short. It wasn't the end because Rahul and Akriti were just about to start the most beautiful ride of their life. They were about to get married.

Epilogue

Rahul's life had eventually brought him where he belonged. Yet there was one thing that still remained to be done in order to do justice to his past. A couple of days later, he met Trisha, along with Karan, when she was released from the asylum. He not only met her but also apologized for abandoning her. Karan was also sorry from the depth of his heart. You can't come into someone's life full of promises, and then leave suddenly without an explanation. These little but important things might sometimes make an indelible mark on someone's soul, leaving them with questions that cannot be answered. Trisha was surprised to see Rahul and Karan after years. She had moved on from her tragedy and had completely recovered. Greeting them with a smile, she accepted their apologies. Rashi and her parents were

overjoyed to see Trisha smiling. Rashi embraced her
younger sister. She had missed her so much, then she
smiled forgivingly at Rahul, and Rahul smiled back.

Stories end, situations change, people get accustomed
to new situations, and you know what? Life goes on.
Rashi had decided to make up for the time she couldn't
be with Trisha by showing her how the city had changed
with time. Even after years, they shared the same level
of bonding, and once again, they became each other's
strength. There was no better sister than Rashi and no
better friend than Trisha. Eventually, Rashi got married,
but not to Karan, and although she stayed at her
husband's home, they would visit Trisha every weekend
at her parents' house. They would laugh together at their
childhood vows.

On the other hand, Karan made his parents realize
that even though Rahul had been a little rebellious as a
child, their way of dealing with him had been too harsh.
Karan also made them understand that it was important
to adjust to the changing times. Adjustment did not mean
forfeiting their values and moral principles, it simply
meant becoming flexible to accommodate the younger
generation and their ideas. His parents, after listening to
Rahul's part of the story and Karan's words, realized their
folly. For the time Rahul stayed in Mumbai, his parents
treated him kindly and with respect. For the first time

in his life, he felt like he had come home. In a way, that was Karan's priceless gift to Rahul on Rahul's marriage.

After the wedding, Rahul shifted back to Delhi and resumed work once his suspension orders were cancelled. Rahul and Akriti bought an apartment in Delhi where they began a new phase of their lives together. What about Neerav? He's still single and Rahul still mocks him by saying, 'You'll stay single all your life. Only I can handle you and no one else. I am your one true love.' When Rahul was booking his honeymoon tickets to Phuket, he even mockingly asked Neerav if he wanted to join them, like he always did.

'Of course, I will come!' Neerav exclaimed unabashedly, 'don't forget Maddy always follows Suppandi.' ☺

Acknowledgements

All the people I thank below were my strength while I was writing the book.

My millions of readers for their unflinching love and support! You mean the world to me.

Jasmine Sethi, my soulmate and the only person who injects immense positivity in me and stands by me through thick and thin.

Dipika Tanna, my BFF, who has always supported me.

Zankrut Oza, for guiding me patiently and for his brotherly love.

All the people who really matter—Mom, Dad, my sister, Shweta, and my grandparents for believing in me.

God for being kind to me when it comes to writing.

My extended family on Facebook, Twitter and Instagram who selflessly promote the book.

Milee Ashwarya, Gurveen Chadha, Shruti Katoch and the whole team at Penguin Random House for their patience during the entire process of the book.